FAITH IS NOT
SILENT

ENDORSEMENTS

Most people see grave stones as the end of a story, but for Billie Fulton they became the beginning of a discovery that will delight your heart. I've known Billie for years and her creativity never stops amazing me! She's an engaging story teller who weaves hope and inspiration through every page.

—Jennifer Rothschild, author of *Lessons I Learned in the Dark* and *Me, Myself and Lies*, founder, Fresh Grounded Faith Events and *The 4:13 Podcast*.

I love cemeteries. Many people fail to realize cemeteries are for the living as well as the dead. Research and imagination can make cemeteries come alive. This is precisely what Billie has done. From a small graveyard on their farm, she fashioned a living world, a fascinating landscape alive with stories, memories, dreams, events, and lessons to be learned.

After you read this book, you will view the people buried on the Fulton farm as lives that mattered. You will respect them—yes love them—and, like me, will want to visit the cemetery on Fulton Farm.

—Dr. John E. Marshall, Retired Pastor of Second Baptist Church, Springfield, Missouri

I've walked the land. I have photographed the monuments that stood silent and forgotten on the Fulton Farm until now. Thankfully, Billie Fulton's inspired writing brings to life a buried story that would have been lost forever in a lonely cemetery in Lawrence County, Missouri. Fulton's inspiring saga that chronicles the determination of pioneer businesswoman, Frances Crawford, her patriotic family and her famous American patriot friends will live forever in the minds of the readers!

—Darrel Campbell, author, filmmaker, Percussion Films.

Billie has penned a beautifully written story, a story that will touch your heart. I was sorry when I turned the last page.

—Lori Copeland, bestselling author and national speaker.

The Fultons did more than preserve an old burial ground. In this inspiring, heartfelt story of discovery and faith, Billie Fulton has brought the people behind the stones to life through historical facts and fiction. In

Faith is Not Silent, we are able to enter the Catts and Crawford families' lives and hearts and experience with them joy, grief, love, and faith during the tumultuous times in our nation's history.

—**Kathy Fairchild**, Lawrence County Historical Society Museum Chairman

As a great-great-grandson of Frances (Neal) Catts, I greatly appreciate the interest in and research of my family by the Fultons. They found documentation and confirmation of many of the family stories my dad passed to me verbally and details I had not known before, such as who in the family had been a playmate of Francis Scott Key. I'm delighted Billie wove my family history and Christian heritage into her book.

—**Major C. William L. Catts**, United States Air Force, Retired, great-great-grandson of Francis (Neal) Catts Crawford

We are so thankful and proud of Billie and John Fulton's exhaustive effort to investigate, compile, and write the story of the Crawford family's service to these United States of America.

—**C.M. and Nelda Crawford**, Calvary Commander United States Army, Retired, great-great-grandson of Colonel Robert W. Crawford.

FAITH IS NOT
SILENT

Billie Fulton
ILLUSTRATED BY JOHN FULTON

PUBLISHING THE POSITIVE

ELK LAKE PUBLISHING INC.
Plymouth, Massachusetts

Cover and Interior Design: Derinda Babcock

Editor(s): Deb Haggerty

Illustrations: John Fulton

PUBLISHED BY: Elk Lake Publishing, Inc., 35 Dogwood Dr., Plymouth, MA 02360, 2018

Library Cataloging Data

Names: Fulton, Billie (Billie Fulton)

Faith Is Not Silent / Billie Fulton

230 p. 23cm × 15cm (9in × 6 in.)

Description: A cemetery in the middle of a hayfield, forgotten until a young boy asked the question, "Who were these people?" So starts the saga of the Catts/Crawford family—now to be remembered by all who read their story.

Identifiers: ISBN-13: 978-1-948888-57-8 (trade) | 978-1-948888-58-5 (POD)

Key Words: History, Family, Legacy, Ancestors, Civil War, Antiques, Oregon Trail

LCCN: 2018956803 Fiction

DEDICATION

To God who saved me.
To my husband John, who gives me unending love and encouragement.
To our daughters and son-in-law's who cover us with prayer
To our grandchildren who are the future stories of faith and honor.

ACKNOWLEDGMENTS

I especially want to thank our grandson, Tate, who asked the simple questions, "Who?" and "Why?" Your innocent curiosity allowed me to find my friend, Francis Neal Catts Crawford, a lady I grew to admire and wanted to learn from.

To John, my husband. Your encouragement and love from the beginning to the end of our journey with the book has given me joy all the way to the finish line. Your faith, which is never silent, has given me guidance when I needed it most. I will love you forever.

To Tate, Lydia, Pru, Silas, and Priscilla. You have all kept me dancing in the bubbles when I needed a break. Your creative minds gave me new ideas to build the characters. And each of your personalities are hidden somewhere in the book for you to find. And to your parents, Kelli, Jason, Cassi, and Chad. Thank you for your loving support and for reminding me that all things are possible with God. I will love you all forever.

To Deb Haggerty, Publisher and Editor-in-Chief, at Elk Lake Publishing, Inc. You told me my story had "good bones," and to keep writing. Your wisdom and guidance helped me all the way to the last page. Thank you for your exceptional gift of encouragement.

To Derinda Babcock, graphic designer for Elk Lake. You astonished me with your creativity and your responsiveness. Thank you for your suggestions and help making the illustrations fit within my words.

To Jeanne Marie Leach, Editor and Writing Coach. Thank you for your prayers as you guided me through each chapter and all the way to the end. I'm so very thankful for you.

To Bill Catts and C.M. Crawford, great-great grandsons of the Catts/Crawford family. Your kindness and helpfulness to provide family stories and family history helped me find the heart of the seven people buried in our hayfield. Although written as fiction, your information laid the foundation for the real people and real events in history that touched their lives. Thank you for allowing your family to touch my life with their faith and their honor. You have a family heritage to be proud of that continues with you today.

To Michelle Sauter Cox. I am thankful you invited me to the Blue Ridge Mountain Christian Writers Conference. I now realize you truly do know everybody.

To my neighbor and friend Barbara Philips. I am grateful to you and your writing group for their support and encouragement.

To Jeff Patrick with Wilson Creek National Battlefield. Thank you for helping me research the Catts Crawford family's involvement in the Civil War.

To Marty Blevins. Your funny stories about the Fulton Farm gave me a new perspective on farm life. Thank you my friend.

PROLOGUE

An old cemetery lies in the middle of a hayfield on our family farm in Missouri. For a century and a half, seven souls have lain forgotten in silence.

Since they weren't our family members, we'd never researched who the people were or where they came from. We knew from county documents they were the original homestead family. Perhaps out of respect and responsibility, our family cleaned the cemetery once a year. Chiggers and ticks were always our unfortunate reward.

But the tiny cemetery had been like a silent city all this time, waiting for someone to ask the question that would finally give its inhabitants the opportunity to tell their story.

Sweet-smelling spring flowers were in bloom as Memorial Day approached, and once again the time to clean the forgotten cemetery arrived.

We never could have foreseen the chain of events that occurred that day when our ten-year-old grandson asked the simplest questions that began our journey to discover the hearts of seven people.

PART I

CHAPTER 1

For where your treasure is, there your heart will be also. (Matthew 6:21)

Ten-year-old Tate Ledbetter was spending a few days with his grandparents, Pops and Grams, at the farm. His parents had decided a little hard work might help him adjust his attitude about what was bothering him.

Pops told Tate he was happy to spend time with him, and he'd planned some projects for them to accomplish. "Projects" usually involved work.

And sure enough. On his first full day there, with a cool morning breeze, blue skies above, and a carpet of cut green grass to walk on in the hayfield, Pops, Grams, and Tate headed out to the little cemetery like soldiers on a mission. Prepared with a bucket of tools, their goal soon came into sight—a year's worth of brush and sky-high weeds. Towering oak trees encircled the cemetery in the hayfield like a hedge of protection.

Tate wasn't too excited to begin their work of pulling weeds, cutting brush, and trimming tree limbs.

As he approached the fence, a huge flock of blackbirds flapped their wings and flew out from the trees, cawing their warnings to one another. Startled by the sound, he looked up and watched them fly away. Huge clouds that looked like snow-capped mountains were gathering southwest of the pond.

"Those clouds will soon deliver rain," Pops said. "Let's get our work done."

Tate didn't think the clouds looked that bad. As he reached for the latch on the rusty gate to the cemetery, a couple rabbits ran away, and he heard other small critters scurrying through the tall grasses. A big, shiny blackbird landed on the fence near him, then another and another. More blackbirds came, making a full circle on the edge of the fence as if they were guards on watch over the cemetery.

They scared him, and he hesitated. Noticing a metal sign welded to the fence, he announced, "Catts/Crawford Cemetery, Established 1854." Then  looking to the left of the gate, he saw a moss-covered cedar plank sign. Unable to read the words from where he stood, he picked up a stick to shoo away the blackbirds and to outline the letters.

Stepping closer to the sign, he knocked away the moss and read aloud:

"Charles H. Crawford
Beloved son of Thomas and Frances Crawford
Born 1831, Wellsburg, Virginia
Died May 21, 1858, Honey Lake, California."

Pops said, "I found that old sign in the corner of the cemetery years ago. I guess someone in the family made it for Charles since he isn't buried here. I hung the  sign on the fence, so he wouldn't be forgotten.

Tate touched a metal cross wired to the gate. Still pondering  who Charles Crawford might have been, he pushed up the latch on the side of the gate. Suddenly, a strong wind pushed the gate open wide. Without hesitation, Tate stepped into the cemetery. Once inside, a good feeling settled over him.

Pops hung the tool bucket on the fencepost. "Grab a pair of those work gloves from the bucket," he said to Tate and Grams, "and start pulling those tall weeds over there. I'll cut the small brush in the center and work my way outward to the fence."

Tate sighed. This was going to be a long day. He and Grams grabbed their gloves and soon piled armloads of weeds and brush in the corner near a tree. Finally, they cleared away enough weeds that they could see seven gravestones—four standing tall and three that lay broken on the ground.

Sweat rolling down her face, Grams went back to the tool bucket. She pulled out a wide roll of white paper, a soft cleaning brush, and a box of big, black, flat crayons, and then walked toward one of the graves.

Tate watched her curiously. What do crayons have to do with cleaning the graveyard? She wasn't going to color the gravestones, was she?

Bending down, Grams got on her knees beside one of the broken gravestones. Pushing the pieces together and brushing away the dirt with the brush, she motioned for Tate and Pops to help. She unrolled a long piece of paper and laid it flat on top of the broken pieces.

Pops got down on one knee, and Tate knelt beside him in the dirt. Pops showed him how to rub the flat crayon over the gravestone.

"It is called a rubbing," Grams said to Tate with a smile on her face.

He continued to rub harder with the crayon, and soon, letters appeared on the paper.

"Frances Crawford," Tate read aloud. Rubbing farther down the paper, he read the words: "Wife of T. Crawford, Born February 8, 1792, Died, April 24, 1890." He never expected the graves to be so old. "Wow!" he exclaimed. Counting by tens, he did the math using his fingers and was amazed that someone born that long ago would be buried on the farm. "She was born two hundred twenty-six years ago and lived to be ninety-eight years old!"

Excited, Tate moved to the next gravestone, unrolling more paper as he went.

Pops kept glancing up at the clouds as they worked. "We need to hurry. Those clouds are getting darker and closer." He hurried to finish cleaning the cemetery while Grams and Tate made gravestone rubbings.

They finished the last rubbing and quickly rolled them up together. Gathering their tools, they walked toward the open gate.

Abruptly stopping, Tate looked back at each grave, curious and confused. He asked, "Grams, who are these people, and why did they get buried in the middle of a hayfield?"

"We'd better run," Pops called out. "I can smell the rain. The storm's getting close."

He grabbed his tool bucket off the fencepost, and Grams tucked the gravestone rubbings under her shirt.

They ran across the hayfield toward a gate that opened to the lane leading up to the white, two-story farm house. Hearing rain drops begin to dance on the nearby pond, Tate ran ahead to open the gate. By making bigger, faster strides, they reached the steps of the white-railed porch as the clouds opened up a downpour of rain.

Waiting on the porch was fuzzy-faced Wooster, Pops' farm dog.

Winded, Tate bent over and supported himself with his hands on his knees, and Pops and Grams leaned against the porch rail to catch their breath.

"Is anybody hungry?" Grams said. "I'll go make us some lunch." She headed inside, and Tate was about to follow her.

"Would you sit with me on the porch swing, Tate?" Pops asked him.

"Sure, Pops," he answered. He'd grown up sitting on the swing with Pops.

"I thought while Grams is busy, we could talk man to man." They made themselves comfortable on the swing. "What's been going on with you lately?"

First, Tate discussed how unfair his parents had been to him and how his sister never seemed to get in trouble, only him. For ten minutes, his complaints flowed from him like a swift stream.

Pops listened to all of Tate's gripes without interruption.

Finally, Tate felt he could confide in Pops what was really bothering him. "A few weeks ago, a friend of mine named Rocky died of cancer. I prayed for over a year for God to heal him. Then he suddenly got worse and died." He looked up at Pops, tears forming in his eyes. "I got mad at God. And I'm still mad at God for not healing Rocky." Tears ran down Tate's cheeks as he buried his head against Pops. No words could have comforted him at that moment. Pops pulled him close with his strong arm while Tate grieved for his friend from his hurting heart.

Slowly swinging back and forth in silence, they listened as the rain drops hit the tin roof on the barn east of the house. A frozen moment in time Tate knew he would never forget. How he loved his Pops.

The rain continued pouring down through lunch. Their plans for doing anything outside would have to be changed.

Tate helped Grams with the dishes, and then she turned to him with a sparkle in her eyes. "For a long time now, I've wanted to clean the attic. After Pops' parents passed away, we moved into the farmhouse, and I never had time to sort through the old trunks and boxes in the attic." She drained the dishwater and rinsed out the sink. "You never know what we might find up there … maybe even some sort of treasure."

Treasure sounded interesting.

"We planned ahead and had the attic sprayed for bugs and spiders."

He'd never been in the attic, so Tate asked if he could see where they'd be working. "Sure you can," Grams replied and walked over to the stairway door.

She opened the door to the wooden steps that led to the second floor of the farm house. Excited to see what was in the attic, he took the stairs two at a time, all the way to the top. Grams and Pops followed closely behind.

Upstairs were three bedrooms, one above the porch, one to the left, and another to the right.

Grams went into the bedroom on the right and turned on a lamp.

Glancing around the room, Tate saw a short wooden door in the corner.

Pops walked over to the door, pressed down on the thumb latch and shoved the door open. They were greeted by a musty smell that drifted out from the attic.

Ducking his head low, he entered the dark attic. Once inside, he was able to stand up where the two sides of the roof joined into a peak. A single light bulb hung from the rafter. He pulled a chain and the light came on.

Holding firm to his position at the threshold of the attic door, Tate cautiously peeked inside. He saw cobwebs in every direction, old trunks, boxes, suitcases, broken crates of old jars, and baskets hanging from hooks. He slowly stepped inside, feeling like an explorer in a long-forgotten sealed room of a museum.

He could see a gray stone chimney toward the back wall of the attic. Behind the chimney, more things were tucked and shoved in the corners.

"Ow!" Pops exclaimed.

Tate turned and laughed when he realized Pops had bumped his head on the hanging light bulb that now swung like a pendulum, back and forth. Light danced around the attic and shadows bounced across the rafters and side walls. His heart jumped inside his chest. He stepped backward and fell against the gray stone chimney. Trying to catch his balance, he reached up to grab an extended stone to stop his fall. The stone dislodged and fell forward and Tate fell with it.

Pops reached down to help him stand to his feet. He wasn't hurt, except for his pride. Looking for the hole where the stone fell out, he saw something shiny. "Pops, what is that?"

"I don't know," he replied. Taking out his pocket knife, Pops used it to pull the shiny object forward. A brass ring with keys attached fell with a jingling crash to the floor.

Shocked they'd found something hidden away, Tate picked up the keys.

"Is everything all right in here?" Grams asked as she entered the attic room. When she saw the ring of keys in Tate's hand, she asked, "What's that? Where did they come from?"

"We found them inside the chimney when I leaned on this stone," Tate said with excitement in his voice. "The stone came loose and left this hole. See?" He pointed out the missing spot in the chimney where the rock once resided.

"Hmm," she said. "What do you think those open?"

"I don't know," Pops said. "The fact they were hidden might mean something important."

"You mean, like a treasure?" Tate asked, opening his eyes wide as his heart beat faster.

"Maybe," Grams answered. She looked around the attic. "I didn't realize how mammoth a job cleaning and sorting all this  stuff would be." She picked up an old wooden box with a cross carved on the top and handed it to Tate. "Here's your first treasure to open," she told him, and she ducked her head to leave the attic.

Pops looked at Tate and said, "Maybe you'll find what those keys unlock inside that box."

Tate nodded. Pops pulled the chain to turn out the light, and with the keys and box in hand, Tate pulled the attic door closed.

When they all got down to the kitchen, Grams placed an old oilcloth on one side of the breakfast table along with some cleaning rags.

"I wonder who hid the keys and why they hid them." Tate laid the keys and the box on the oil cloth.

Smearing layers of dust around with his fingers, Tate rubbed the cross carved on top of the box. Grams handed him a rag, and he wiped his hands, fingers, and the box. He turned the box over. Carved on the bottom were the initials, "J. N." He then looked up at Pops for approval before lifting the top of the wooden box.

Pops' face looked as anxious as Tate felt, and he nodded.

Slowly, Tate opened the box as the rusty hinges made a creaking sound. Leaning forward, they all three stared at what was inside.

"A book!" Tate exclaimed. Again, he looked at Pops for his approval. Carefully, he lifted the book from the box and placed it on the oil cloth.

Gently touching the cracked black-leather book, Tate traced the large gold letters that spelled out *Holy Bible*.

Then he read smaller gold letters near the bottom. "Who are the Catts Family?"

Looking from one to the other, Pops and Grams shrugged their shoulders.

"Could this belong to the family buried in the hayfield?" Grams asked.

Slowly opening the Bible, she read the inscription written in swirling old-fashioned script, "To our beloved, John William Catts and Frances Neal Catts, September 20, 1810." She looked up at Pops and Tate. "Maybe this was a wedding gift." She thumbed through the Bible as if she were looking for something, then she handed the book to Pops to look at.

He opened it and showed Tate detailed story illustrations of Bible stories. Turning to the center between the Old and New Testaments, he stopped. With a shocked look on his face, he looked up at Grams and Tate.

"What's the matter?" Grams and Tate asked at the same time.

Pops laid the Bible open on the table and pointed to a list of names and dates, all in hand-scrolled writing.

"It's the Catts/Crawford family records," Pops said boldly.

Tate rolled his eyes and then raised his eyebrows when a thought suddenly came to him. Without saying a word, he turned and walked away. He went to the table with the gravestone rubbings and unrolled one after another on the table and on the floor.

Realizing what Tate was doing, Pops looked at the first rolled-out rubbing. He called out, "Frances, Beloved Wife of T. Crawford, Born February 8, 1792, Died April 24, 1890."

Barely able to contain herself, Grams shouted, "Her name is listed in the Bible!"

Tate hurried to the second rubbing rolled out on the table and called out, "George Neal Catts, Born February 13, 1812."

"His name is in the Bible too," Grams said in an excited voice.

Already at the third rubbing, Pops read, "Mary Ann Catts, Born February 1, 1821."

"She's here," Grams replied.

One by one, Tate and Pops called out the remaining names from the rubbings: Fannie M. Catts, Born 1840, Thomas L. Catts, Born 1817, Robert W. Crawford, Born 1812 and Jane Ann Crawford, Born 1813.

They were all listed in the Bible.

Checking once more to be sure all names were in the list, they sat speechless for a few minutes.

Still thinking about the list in the Bible, Tate picked up the keys from the attic and started cleaning them. Suddenly he stopped. Walking around the table, he counted seven rubbings. Still in his hand, he counted seven keys. Thoughts ran like a rushing river through his mind. "Do you suppose there could be some sort of connection between the keys and the people who lived and died on this farm?" he said aloud to himself.

"With a key comes responsibility," Pops voice broke through Tate's thoughts. "Whether the key's for a car, a door, or something from someone's past. When you find what the key opens, you have to decide what to do with the contents and assume the responsibly for them."

Suddenly, they all started to talk at once. Now, they wanted to know more about the family buried in the hayfield.

Maybe staying with Grams and Pops wouldn't be so bad after all.

Tate and Pops spent the afternoon searching local history and the places where the family members were born.

"This is fun," Tate told his grandparents. "It's like a treasure hunt."

"I think it's more like a treasure hunt into history," Pops said.

"I'm glad it's a treasure hunt in the attic that I wanted cleaned." Grams added.

Digging into old farm records of his Dad's, Pops found a copy of the original homestead papers to the farm. Tucked here and there were handwritten notes and copies of wills pertaining to the land.

Helping with the search, Grams diligently looked through each page of the Bible. Between some of the pages, she found letters and family obituaries.

"I've got an idea," Pops said. "Let's make a timeline chart of each life." He got out the roll of white paper that Grams had used for the rubbings and showed Tate how to list each name, date of birth, and where each was born. They included all the information they found in their research.

They worked on their new project throughout the afternoon.

After supper Tate, Pops, and Grams went out on the front porch to "watch the pond." Grams' red geraniums were in full bloom, and the evening breeze gently lifted the American flag that hung on a porch post.

Looking at the rolling fields beyond the pond, Tate said, "I wonder what life was like when the Catts/Crawford family lived on the farm."

"The history of the land is what you need to imagine first, Tate," Pops responded. He waved his arms over the land in an arcing motion. "Long ago, buffalo roamed these fields, and to this day, there's a place in the woods my Dad called the buffalo wallow. During spring rains, a low area would fill with water and turn into mud. The huge buffalo would come here to roll in the thick mud to comfort their lice-infested hides and to cool their massive bodies. Covered in mud, the male buffalos would rise and make snorting sounds to show their strength and to challenge other males.

"I want you to fully understand the history of the land," Pops continued. "American Indians also roamed these fields. Their families needed the meat of the buffalo for food. So, where the buffalos roamed, the Indians followed. In the woods, ten-foot-wide mounds of soil show where Indians placed their teepees so rain would drain away from where they slept. Many Osage and Kickapoo Indians hunted this land and raised their families here. Broken pottery and arrowheads can still be found around the Indian mounds where they camped."

Tate loved the story Pops told him. It helped him understand the land. He'd never thought about Indians living on the farm.

"Thick brush and woodlands use to cover the farm," Pops continued. "It was called undeveloped wild land. There were no fences, no houses, and no crops. To help develop the land as America expanded west, our government offered free land to families willing to *homestead*."

"What's homestead mean?" Tate asked.

"They were required to move here, register a plot of one hundred sixty acres with the land office. Then they had to live on the land, build a house, and plant crops."

Tate asked, "Was that when the Catts/Crawford family moved onto the land to make it their home?"

"Yes, and that is where their story begins." Pops smiled.

Thinking about all he had learned in just one day, Tate sat quietly with Pops and Grams. They watched the ducks paddle around in circles looking for bugs and minnows in the pond and listened as the bullfrogs croaked back and forth in harmony.

Tate stretched as he stood up and reached to give Grams and Pops a goodnight hug.

Turning to go inside, he jingled the keys he'd put in his pocket and let himself smile in anticipation of what the new day would bring. "Tomorrow, we'll find more treasures in the attic," he said and headed to bed.

He got into his pajamas and crawled between the sheets, his mind still racing. He thought about his friend, Rocky. Thankful he'd talked to Pops, he was beginning to understand some of what he'd been feeling. He must have been bothered more than he'd thought. The strange thing was, he didn't feel quite so angry anymore.

His thoughts turned to the cemetery, the rubbings, and the old Bible in the wooden box. He reached over to the nightstand and touched the keys. A real-life treasure hunt awaited him in the morning. What treasures would the keys unlock? How would he ever sleep tonight?

CHAPTER 2

Pitching the polished brass keys up and down in his hands, Tate walked into the kitchen with a smile and a big appetite. Pops was already sitting at the table, and he sat down beside him. The aromas flowing from a large platter stacked high with golden-brown vanilla pancakes and crispy hickory-smoked bacon captured his attention.

Grams set a pitcher of hot syrup on the table and joined them.

Tate reached for some pancakes when Grams touched his hand. "We need to pray first."

When they finished the prayer, the feasting began.

"I've been up early looking through old farm documents for clues about the Catts/Crawford family," Pops said as he piled his plate with pancakes and bacon.

Tate stopped his fork in midair. "Did you find anything else?"

"I realized I'd forgotten about some people who came by here years ago, looking for their family," Pops said as he gazed toward the west kitchen window. "A nice man from Texas named Mr. Crawford came searching for the grave of his great-great-grandfather and great-grandfather."

"Were they in our cemetery?" Tate asked then shoved a bite of pancakes drenched in syrup into his mouth.

Pops gave a smile when Tate said *our*. "Looking through county records, he found the grave of his great-great-grandfather, Thomas Crawford, at the Neely Cemetery three miles west of here. As it turned out, his great-grandfather was Robert W. Crawford, who's buried in the hayfield. His great-grandmother was Jane Ann Catts Crawford, who's buried beside Robert Crawford."

"I knew it!" Tate said, nodding.

"Concerned about vandals who'd used bats to break three of the gravestones in years past, Mr. Crawford wanted a permanent fence put around the graves. I agreed it needed to be done. So, arrangements were made, and the fence was installed. He's the one who arranged for the sign to be welded onto the fence to identify the cemetery.

"There was another nice man, Mr. Catts, who was in the military for much of his life. He came looking for his great-grandfather, George Neal Catts's, grave. He not only found that one, but also his great grandmother, Mary Ann Tarr Catts. And he found his great-great-grandmother's grave, Frances Neal Catts Crawford. Mr. Catts was the one who placed the cross on the gate.

"Both the Catts and Crawford families were people with deep faith in God. They didn't allow their faith to be silent in their family, in their community, and in the decisions they made.

"Mr. Catts, also a man of faith, attached the cross on the gate as an identity marker of their Christian heritage. He lived far away for many years and was unable to come to the cemetery. He left the cross for future generations who might come searching for family."

"But if they already knew where their relatives were buried, why would someone need to come searching for them?" Tate asked.

"Well, some things are often not thought about and can be forgotten, like the cemetery. Someone might forget to tell their children about the graves of their ancestors. It happens."

Tate understood. He finished his breakfast quickly and sat there impatiently.

Finally, Pops laid down his fork and nodded to him. "Ready?"

"Yeah!" Tate checked to be sure the keys were in his pocket, even though he knew they were. Anxious to get started cleaning the attic, he raced up the steps ahead of Pops to begin their treasure hunt.

Grams went up the steps behind the two guys. Spreading out old sheets and blankets in the floor and on the bed in the room to the right, she prepared for their work.

Pops had brought a toolbox in case they needed tools and a notebook to document the treasures they might find.

Tate had a pocket full of keys and a heart for adventure.

Stepping inside the attic, Pops turned on the hanging light bulb and shook his head as he looked at the junk stacked every direction. A hammered metal camelback trunk was the first thing he passed out of the attic door to Tate.

Grams pulled the trunk against the wall and stacked hat boxes from the attic on top. Then more and more came out of the attic, including a brown leather suitcase.

Noticing a lock on the suitcase, Tate pulled the keys from his pocket and tried to insert one of them into the lock, but it wouldn't fit. He tried a second key, then a third. Finally, the fourth key turned, and the lock sprang open.

"It works!" he shouted, and Grams and Pops came and stood beside him as he opened the suitcase. There were no clothes inside, but it was filled with curious objects.

The first thing he pulled from the suitcase was a rusty metal cash box with dirt pressed on the corners. Tate looked over at Pops.

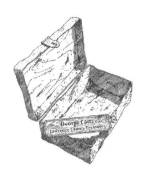

"Go ahead and open it."

Puzzled as to why anyone would save the rusted box, Tate looked inside, pulled out a wooden sign and read, "George Neal Catts, County Treasurer, Lawrence County, Missouri." No treasure there, but Pops wrote the information down in his notebook anyway.

Next, he pulled out a black ledger with "Mount Vernon Mercantile" inscribed on the front. Opening the hard cover, Tate read, "George and Mary Ann Catts, Owners, Established September 9, 1852." He looked up. "They're buried in the cemetery."

Again, Pops wrote down the information.

Tate next picked up a small clothbound book titled *Latin Reader*. Looking at a list of names on the inside, he recognized the names of George N. Catts, Robert W. Crawford, and Thomas L. Catts. The names were becoming familiar to him.

Wedged in the corner of the suitcase

was a square cherrywood box with beautiful scrolled lettering. Speaking loudly enough so Grams and Pops could hear, Tate dramatically read, "To my sweet Mary Ann." *G. C. and M. A.* were inside a carved heart, and underneath the heart was the word *forever.*

Grams and Pops peeked over Tate's shoulder to see the box. Pops pointed to a lock, showing him that the scrolling on one of the keys matched the scrolling on the lock. Tate inserted and turned the key, and the box opened. His heart did a flip-flop.

Inside was a stack of tattered, yellowed letters tied together with a faded ribbon. Grams suggested they read them later since they might be personal notes between Mary Ann and George. Underneath was a soft blue crocheted piece used as wrapping. Carefully, she

helped Tate unwrap one white china plate. Pretty, kind of like his mom's good china. He set the plate down carefully on the side table.

In the corner of the box, wrapped in the same crocheting, was a small item. Pops held the article in his big hands while Tate pulled the wrapping away, revealing a beautiful china box with a pink rose painted on top.

Pops turned the box over where he found a winding stem. He asked Tate to hand him the oil from his tool box. Gently twisting the stem back and forth a little at a time, he put drops of oil around the stem.

The music box came to life and tinkled out a melody.

Grams hummed the tune and then started to sing, "Mary Had A Little Lamb."

When Pops turned the china box back over, a heart-shaped locket fell open to the floor. All three of them looked down at the tiny faded face of a man staring up at them.

Pops recorded each item found in the suitcase and showed Tate the initials *G.N.C.* on the front of the luggage.

"It must be George Catts'," Tate said quietly.

Grams unfolded the soft, blue crocheted pieces. Holding them up, she said, "They're a handmade baby sweater and hat."

Putting the pieces back into the suitcase, they agreed anything opened with one of the seven keys should be placed together in the other bedroom. With the hope that more locks would be found, they pulled more items from the attic.

Pops had Tate help him carry a cedar chest through the small attic door. Tate's eyes danced when he saw a lock on the front of the chest. The moment after they set the piece down, Tate had his keys in hand. Already having marked the two keys he'd used, he tried the next two on the ring. The third key turned but got stuck. Tate wiggled the key back and forth, and the lock finally opened.

"Just look at the master craftsmanship of this cedar chest," Pops said, capturing Tate's attention. He pointed out to Tate the brass nail heads, the hammered-brass corners, the curved legs, and the oval brass plate across the front.

Rubbing the plate with the corner of his shirt, Tate saw the name, *Fannie*, engraved on the brass. He delighted at the thought the chest probably belonged to Fannie Catts, whose name was in the Bible and on a gravestone in the cemetery.

Grams raised the top of the chest.

Tate stood right beside her. Inside was some neatly folded white lace. "What beautiful handmade lace," she said, gently

lifting the material. The folds fell open and revealed a wedding dress. Grams swirled the dress up over the trunk, held it up in front of her, and gracefully waltzed over to a mirror. "I wonder who wore this at her wedding."

Not interested in a dress, Tate looked deeper into the chest. He pulled out an old book titled, "The Shepherd of the Hills," and handed it to Pops.

Pops opened the book and looked at the first page. "This is a first edition signed copy!" Showing Tate, Pops reads, "To my dear friend Fannie, I pray God will bless and keep you. Your friend, Harold Bell Wright." Several old-time photographs of Wright and a lady with school children were tucked into the back of the book.

Tate kept looking in the chest, hoping to find something more interesting. He handed Grams a colorful folded quilt and a white lace purse.

 Unfolding the quilt, she told him, "It's a Friendship Quilt. See?" She opened the quilt on the bed. "There are twelve square embroidered blocks of fabric, and each block is embroidered with a flower and a girl's name."

Grams explained to Tate that twelve of Fannie's friends each embroidered a block, probably as a gift for her. She later sewed the blocks together to make the quilt. Pulling the bottom of the quilt up for Tate to see words embroidered in pink, he read, "Make new friends but keep the old; one is silver and the other is gold."

Opening the lace purse, Grams found a hand-written poem. She read the verse aloud as the guys continued to rummage through the stuff.

FAITH IS NOT SILENT

Love Did Not Pass Me By

Oh, what a beautiful summer sky
On the day that war did not pass me by.
The clouds were so magnificent that day.
As I sat on the porch, I began to pray.

Up the road my true love came, sitting tall in his saddle,
To tell me he's leaving to fight an emanate battle.
My heart hurt oh so deeply as we said our goodbyes.
I told him, "I promise I will love you until the day that I die."

I watched him ride away until I could see him no more;
In my soul I knew he would not return from this day of war.
My sweet memories I've held for such a long while
Of his handsome face and his radiant smile.

Beautiful puffy clouds on hot summer days,
Always reminds me of the day my true love went away.
But I believe it's God who chooses who will live and who will die,
So, I choose to be thankful that love did not pass me by.

As a tear rolled down her cheek, Grams whispered, "She never got to wear this beautiful dress."

"He must have gone to fight in the battle at Wilson Creek during the Civil War," Pops added. "She may never have seen him again."

Pops asked Tate to go with him downstairs to make lunch.

"But why—"

Pops shook his head and put his forefinger against his lips.

Tate quietly followed his grandfather downstairs. When they got to the kitchen, he asked, "Why isn't Grams making lunch? What's she doing up there?"

"You'll learn soon enough that God gave people—women especially—the ability to feel other's pain and loss. She's sort of grieving over Fannie's loss of her true love," Pops told Tate.

Tate nodded. He thought about Rocky and fought to not choke up. The sooner he helped Pops get lunch ready, the sooner he could get his mind off his friend and get back up into the attic to continue the treasure hunt.

He and Pops went outside and picked some of Grams' red roses and placed them in a vase. "Now, remember, she'll probably still be sad when she comes down to eat," he reminded Tate. "Let's not talk about the attic while we eat, okay?"

"Sure, Pops."

Grams came down to the kitchen shortly after that, but she wasn't sad at all.

Tate looked at Pops, and Pops looked at him. They both shrugged and sat down to eat.

Grams hummed as they followed her back upstairs after lunch. She had the items from Fannie's trunk laid out on the bed for Tate to see—books and letters from children, keepsakes from the 1876 Centennial in Philadelphia and the 1904 World's Fair in St. Louis, and pictures and post cards from monumental events in history.

Opening a record book, she showed Tate how Fannie had collected money to help build the First Christian Church in Mount Vernon.

Then with excitement in her voice, Grams said, "Fannie enjoyed life even with heartache. Evidently, she was at peace when her fiancé didn't come home. She chose to be thankful for the time she had been in love. And when she promised him she would love him until the day she died, she meant her vow."

Grams continued to hum the rest of the afternoon while she worked.

Tate liked the sound, and he began to hum along.

After writing down the items found in Fannie's cedar chest, Pops pulled more things from the attic. In the back corner near the stone chimney, an old leather saddle bag hung from the rafters. He'd hit his head on the bag more than once. After a

final blow to his head, he yanked the bag down and sent it sailing into the bedroom.

As the bag flew past Tate, he couldn't help but notice a lock on the side. Considering himself now a master with locks and keys, he looked at the size of the keyhole and matched a key. The lock opened with the first try.

At that moment, Pops stepped out from the attic, still muttering about the saddle bag hitting him in the head.

Tate held up the bag and the key to show him he'd opened it. The handle was cracked from years of hanging in the hot attic, but the chiseled words across the front were clear.

Pops and Tate read the words in unison. "Robert W. Crawford Esq, Attorney at Law." Tate stumbled over the *Esq.* part, and Pops explained to Tate it indicated Robert was an esquire—another word for lawyer.

Anxious, they opened the now-important saddle bag. Pops held the flap of the bag while Tate pulled out a black Bible with a round hole near the top. Setting the Bible aside, he next took out a book with loose papers on top, tied together with strips of leather, and a trifold, stitched leather wallet.

Wanting to be sure he had everything out of the bag, Tate turned it upside down and gave it a good shake. Two items hit the floor with a thump. Picking them up, he handed the largest one to Pops.

He called the object a shaving razor and showed Tate how it unfolded to open.

Laughing, Pops said, "This will cut the whiskers off any man's face, but if it hasn't been sharpened, it'll scrape the whiskers and the skin off."

Still trying to figure out what the other item might be, Tate laid the object in Pops' hand.

Rolling it around, he said, "This looks like a bullet from a single-shot rifle, perhaps used around the Civil War times. I've seen them in the Museum at Wilson Creek National Battlefield."

Laying aside the bullet, Tate said to Pops, "It must have special meaning for him to have saved it."

Untying the book and papers from Robert Crawford's bag, Pops showed Tate they were court cases and legal files. "I think these can be used to help fill in the timeline of Mr. Crawford's life," he said as he laid them aside.

Picking up the Bible again, Tate opened the worn cover to the first page. He read out loud, "Colonel Robert W. Crawford, July 1861. Soldier's Bible."

He still tried to figure out why it would have a hole. Flipping the Bible over, he realized the hole didn't go all the way through. What could have caused this? Looking at the Bible in one hand and the bullet in the other, he realized the bullet was the same size as the hole. He inserted the bullet into the hole in the Bible. A perfect fit!

Kneeling down beside Tate, Pops said, "The Bible must have been in Robert Crawford's pocket, like this, when he was shot." He placed the book in his shirt pocket. "The Bible protected him by stopping the bullet."

He took the Bible from his pocket and handed the book to Tate. In silent respect, they stared at the Bible in Tate's hand.

Picking up the stitched leather trifold with the letters "R. W. C." on the top, Tate opened the fold. Inside were papers that identified Mr. Crawford, a picture of a lady, and two folded pieces of paper.

"It's an old billfold, Tate," Grams chimed in. "And the picture could be his wife, Jane Ann."

Tate unfolded the paper from the billfold and read out loud:

> To whomever finds this note,
>   If I, Robert W. Crawford, am found dead, please notify my beloved wife, Jane Ann Crawford of Mount Vernon, Missouri. Please tell my family that I deeply loved them until I took my last breath.
>   Robert Wells Crawford
>   July 12, 1861

Tate's eyes unexpectedly glistened with tears. "Did he die?" he asked Pops. Maybe this was what Pops was trying to tell him about how someone could feel bad when something happens to other people you don't even know.

"Tate," Pops replied, "we'll check the family Bible and gravestone rubbing for the date that he died."

Pops unfolded the second note and read, "Place this soldier on the next available medical wagon to Springfield. By command of Colonel Robert Crawford. August 10, 1861."

Not understanding what the note might mean, they placed the saddle bag and its contents on the bed in the other bedroom.

Tate got back to work opening boxes and looking for locks with Robert Crawford still on his mind. He found boxes and boxes of women's hats. This made no sense to him. "Why so many hats?"

"Aren't they beautiful?" Grams said as she gently touched a couple of them. "The braid, the netting, the lace, and the soft tiny pleats in the fabric give such detail to each one."

Some were made of what Grams said was smocked velvet tucked in layers to form a ripple in the front of the hat. Others were of heavy tapestry fabric with wide brims that perhaps were to wear in winter.

"Women wore beautiful dresses back then," Grams said. "And no outfit was complete without a hat, gloves, a matching purse, and sometimes an umbrella, called a parasol."

Grams put on one of the beautiful hats and looked at herself in the mirror above the dresser. Then she closed her eyes for a moment.

What was she thinking about? It must be something nice because she was smiling. Tate had seen Grams daydreaming before. While her eyes were closed, he picked up a black top hat and gestured to Pops to do the same.

When she opened her eyes, she saw Tate and Pops standing before her, wearing the black top hats. The two bowed formally, causing Grams to break out in laughter. They all laughed at themselves as they enjoyed the moment.

Tate wondered why a family of homesteaders would need such fancy hats.

"Well," Grams said as she took off her hat and laid it on the sheet covering the bed. "We won't get much done if we're playing dress-up."

They carefully laid all the hats one by one on a sheet covering the bed.

Still laughing about the hats, Tate sat down on a hammered metal trunk trimmed in oak strips with tarnished brass nail heads. This had been the first thing to come out of the attic and had been hidden by the many hat boxes since then. He was disappointed there was no lock. He hadn't found a match for another of his keys for quite a while.

Tate reluctantly lifted the top of the trunk, thinking it  wouldn't hold anything interesting. To his surprise, he pulled up a sign and read, "Catts Fine Millinery Shop, 63 Lexington Avenue, Baltimore, Maryland."

From inside the attic, Grams said, "That's why there were so many hats! A millinery shop is another name for a hat shop."

Digging deeper in the trunk, Tate called Grams to come to look at a multi-colored quilt.

Unfolding the quilt, Grams announced, "It's a crazy quilt. Fabric was hard to come by in the pioneer days. Mothers used every inch of fabric to make something for their family, and when their clothes wore out, they would cut them up and make quilts out of them."

Unfolding the crazy quilt more, she showed Tate how small and big pieces were sewn together with a brier stitch design to outline the free-flowing lines of each fabric piece.

"What some people thought was nothing was something useful to others. Whoever made this quilt was exceptional at sewing. The tiny stitches and the use of the smallest pieces of fabric to make a beautiful design reveal her talent with a needle."

Again, Pops documented the items.

Gently lifting more things from the trunk, Grams excitedly announced, "And maybe, just maybe, we'll find out who made the quilt."

Tate picked up a tin box and said, "Vassar Chocolates." Opening the box with excitement, he was quickly disappointed.

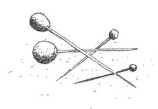

"It's just a bunch of long pins with fancy ends on them."

"They're hat pins," Grams told him. "They were used to embellish or decorate lady's hats as well as to help keep them on their heads."

Down in the bottom of the trunk was a metal box. Picking the small box, Tate saw there was a tiny lock. The sable-brown box displayed a rope design, with rubbed gold and smudges of a turquoise color along the edge. Taking the keys from his pocket, he searched for the smallest. The key and the lock had the same rope design as the box, so he inserted and turned the key, and the lock opened.

Laying on top inside the box was a pair of lady's black gloves with *J. A. C.* embroidered in shiny black thread. Under the gloves was a blue velvet box filled with buttons.

Glancing around the room, Tate spied a clear glass bowl Grams must have found in the attic. From the velvet box, he poured a stream of beautiful glass buttons of every color and shape. They tinkled and danced as they fell into the bowl like jewels for a crown.

Under the velvet box was a small, plain, tin box. Tate poured the contents into Pops' hands. Large tarnished brass buttons fell into his palms. Staring down at them, Tate found one with an emblem of some kind.

"Why, these are from a soldier's Civil War uniform," Pops explained.

The three talked about each item found in the box and in the trunk as they helped Pops record the items.

Tate began to put the pieces together. "Remember that note signed by Colonel Robert W. Crawford we found earlier? I bet these buttons were from Colonel Crawford's uniform, and the gloves belonged to Jane Ann Crawford. She was the hat maker and seamstress. So, the glass buttons, the hat pins, and all these hats were hers."

"I still have two keys I haven't used yet." Determined to find the last two locks, he first looked around the bedroom, and then went back into the attic.

"I'll help you," Pops offered and followed him. He pushed the hanging light bulb from side to side so Tate could see into every corner.

Tate thought he saw a wooden bench pushed against a low rafter in the back of the room. He made his way there, and when he pulled on a side handle, he heard a banging noise. He stopped, and the noise stopped. Pulling again, the noise started again.

"That's odd," Pops said. "Let's get this out into the light so we can see better."

The two pulled the bench into the bedroom so they could better see what was making the noise. On the back side of what they thought was a bench, was a metal lock hitting a metal hasp. Centered on top was a handle. Instead of a bench, it was a wooden box.

"Hmm," Pops said. "I think this is an old tool box."

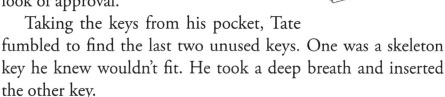

Holding up the lock, Pops gave Tate a look of approval.

Taking the keys from his pocket, Tate fumbled to find the last two unused keys. One was a skeleton key he knew wouldn't fit. He took a deep breath and inserted the other key.

The lock opened. Pops pointed to some letters, *T. L. C.*

Sliding the lock off and lifting the hasp, Tate pushed the wooden box open. Inside was another worn, cracked-leather, Bible lying on top of a board with words carved on one side. Oddly, the board was worn smooth in the middle, almost like a much-used porch step.

Raising the board up, Tate boldly read, "In God is our trust."

Grams walked in just as Tate read the words.

She immediately said, "It's in the fourth verse of our national anthem—"The Star-Spangled Banner." It's a verse we don't sing much anymore. That's also where the words came from that's on our money, *In God We Trust.*"

Grams picked up the Bible, opened the cover, and read a note written there.

In God Is Our Trust

To my dear son: Thomas L. Catts.
May God guide you, protect you, and bring you home safe.
Your loving mother,
Frances Catts Crawford

FAITH IS NOT SILENT

April 15, 1845
Jeremiah 29:11

Grams held the Bible to her heart. "I wonder how Frances must have felt when Thomas left to go west?" she said compassionately.

Searching deeper in the box, Pops found a hunting knife stuck in a leather sheath also with the letters T.L.C., branded on the upper edge. And he found some primitive woodworking tools.

Tate kept digging all the way to the bottom of the dusty old wooden tool box. Pulling out a book with crumpled yellowed papers sticking out the side, he handed it to Pops. So far, all the books they'd pulled out of the attic had some important information in them.

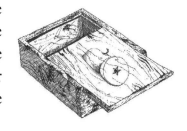

The only thing left in the box was another wooden box—small, with an apple carved on the sliding lid. Looking closer, Tate noticed the apple was carved so the seeds that formed a star in the center of the core could be seen. Sliding the lid open, he found dried seeds.

"What are these for?" he asked.

Grams came closer and peeked inside the box. "Oh, those are apple seeds. People used to save their seeds to start new plants or trees, and so they could share the seeds with their neighbors and family," Grams explained.

Tate nodded. That made sense.

Pops had been going through the book from the box and showed Tate it was a diary about the travels of Thomas Catts on the Oregon Trail going west. And the crumpled papers were

maps marked with crosses on the Oregon Trail that were dated from 1844 to 1849. As he closed the book, a white feather fell to the floor. He picked it up and put the feather back into the book.

Grams cleaned the wooden tool box while Tate and Pops documented the items they found inside.

Still wanting to find what the last key opened, Tate went through everything that had been taken out of the attic but with no success. Pops thought he and Tate should take the list of items found in the attic and fill in as much as possible on the timeline of each person.

They headed downstairs while Grams stayed to clean and box items she wanted to keep in the attic.

The afternoon soon turned into a late evening for Tate and Pops. They continued to research and add information to piece together the seven lives that had been silent for over one hundred and fifty years. The cemetery in the hay field, the silent city, would no longer be silent now that their story could be told.

Tate felt proud to have been a part of piecing together the history of a family who died so long ago. He again thought of his friend, Rocky. As long as people remembered him, Rocky would never be forgotten either.

CHAPTER 3

Tate and Pops searched county records and obituaries about the Catts/Crawford family. Piece by piece, the puzzle of their lives was coming together.

Written above the family records in the Catts/Crawford Bible was the inscription "Faith is not silent, it is eternal." Tate, Pops, and Grams could only imagine the words might have been written by Frances Crawford as a life-long lesson she learned or a statement of wisdom to future generations. Either way, she left the example of her faith for others to find. And they found much more in the attic than ever expected. Also written in the Bible was "In God is our trust."

They searched books and maps, letters and notes, diaries and land records, and the gravestone rubbings, which now were strewn across the dining room table and floor. Timeline charts covered the breakfast table where Grams worked to record all the information.

Completely amazed by the material they were able to compile, Pops suggested they start by writing a short story about the seven people and later add the historic times in each life. He and Tate started the story with Frances.

Frances Neal Catts Crawford
The Story of Seven People Buried in a Hayfield
By Tate Ledbetter

Seven people buried in a hayfield on the Fulton farm in southwest Missouri have been quiet for over one-hundred-fifty years. After finding some items that belonged to them in the attic of the old farm house, ten-year-old Tate Ledbetter wanted to learn more about the seven people. This is a short story about their life that covered one-hundred-eighteen years and is being written two-hundred-and-twenty-six years after Frances Neal Catts Crawford was born.

Frances Neal was born on February 8, 1792, in Baltimore, Maryland. Her parents were Quaker immigrants from England. Her brother was John Neal and her sister was Rachael, twins born in 1793. At age two, Frances developed yellow fever and survived. Her mother taught her God had saved her for a special purpose.

All children at the time were home-schooled, with the Bible used as their main book of learning. Frances was gifted in memorizing and writing Scriptures, often able to quote full chapters from the Bible. She was later called a "scriptorian," a person who stores God's Word in their heart.

The Neal family and Captain John Ross Key's family were close friends. When they and other families got together, the son of Captain Key, Francis Scott Key, would entertain the young children. Frankie, as he was called, would act out Shakespeare, recite poetry, and play games while the parents talked politics.

At age sixteen, Frances fell in love with John Catts, son of Revolutionary War soldier, Michael William Catts. They were married at noon on Independence Day, July 4, 1810. Their first son, George Neal Catts, was born February 13, 1812. Miles away in Wellsburg, Virginia, family friends Thomas and Helen Hammond Crawford had their first son, Robert Wells Crawford on March 3, 1812. George and Robert were born eighteen days apart.

July 12, 1812, the second War of Independence, called the War of 1812, was declared by the United States against the

British. John Catts, Thomas Crawford, and Francis Scott Key all volunteered to serve their country during the war.

Frances gave birth to a daughter while John was at war, Jane Ann Catts, born October 17, 1813.

The war continued, and on August 24, Washington, DC, was burned by the British. Then they moved on to Baltimore, a port city, to take control of all US shipping and trade. John Catts was injured during the battle for Baltimore at Fort McHenry, Thomas Crawford was fighting outside of Baltimore, and Francis Scott Key was being held prisoner on a British ship in the Chesapeake Bay. He watched as his captors aimed every rocket and cannon at the American flag.

The morning after the battle, he saw the flag still flying above the fort, and he wrote the poem that became known as "The Star-Spangled Banner."

Frances gave birth to John Neal Catts, on May 23, 1815, named after her brother, John Neal. And Thomas Love Catts was born on December 6, 1817. Her husband John Catts died from injuries he received during the war on February 28, 1818, at age thirty.

Frances, age twenty-six, was left with four children to bring up alone. Having learned to sew and make hats from her mother, she opened a hat shop in the front half of their house that soon became very successful. Her unmarried sister Rachael moved in with her to help with her children and the hat shop.

Frances's son John Neal died from yellow fever in 1824 at age nine. Frances battled depression after losing her husband and her son while struggling to care for her family.

A widow for eleven years, Frances married family friend, Thomas Crawford, whose wife Helen had passed away, leaving him with four sons to bring up on his own. Frances sold the hat shop to her sister and moved to Wellsburg, Virginia, where

Thomas Crawford, Esq., was a lawyer and an apple orchard farmer.

Frances and Thomas had one son, Charles Hammond Crawford, born 1831. Robert Wells Crawford, son of Thomas and Helen Crawford, married Jane Ann Catts, his stepsister, in 1834. She was the daughter of Frances and John Catts. There was no blood relationship between them. Robert had been away at West Point Military Academy in New York for two years and came home to see beautiful Jane Ann all grown up, so they fell in love.

Thomas Crawford heard there was good farm land to homestead out west in Missouri. After Jane Ann and Robert were married, Thomas, Frances, Charles, and Thomas L. Catts moved to Missouri. George Neal Catts stayed in Virginia, and Thomas's sons kept the apple farm and shared the profits with the rest of the family.

After traveling one thousand miles and living almost four years in either their covered wagon or in a one-room cabin, Thomas Crawford died on September 16, 1838, at Mount Vernon, Missouri. Robert, Jane Ann, and family had moved to Missouri sometime in 1837 to help care for his sick father.

Determined to fulfill Thomas's dream to homestead land in Missouri, Frances stayed in Mount Vernon, filed a claim for land in September 1839, and took possession of one-hundred and sixty acres of farm land. She and her two youngest boys lived in their covered wagon until a one-room cabin could be built from the standing trees on the land. They built a shed for their animals. The next year Thomas L. Catts, now twenty-three, built a house and a barn for his mother and Charles, now age nine.

Wagons trains started rolling west to California on the Oregon Trail. Thomas L. left in 1845 as a wheelwright to make wagon wheels, and then later became a scout on the trail. He made friends with the Indians and carved crosses on trees to communicate with them.

George Catts was still in Virginia and married Mary Ann Tarr in 1839. They had their first baby girl, Fannie Catts, in 1840. After having several other children, Mary Ann, sick throughout her pregnancy, had a premature son, Clarence Catts. The following year, the Catts family moved to Mount Vernon, Missouri, where George opened a mercantile. Unable to gain strength, Little Clarence died in 1854 and was the first person to be buried in the family cemetery on the farm.

Twenty-six-year-old Charles Crawford and a friend took one-thousand head of cattle to California in 1857. The following year Charles died from an Indian arrow wound to his upper leg. His mother, Frances, received a letter saying Charles had died.

In the spring of 1861, the Civil War began. The entire Catts/Crawford family supported the Union. Robert Crawford changed his allegiance in support of state's rights after an incident in Saint Louis. He was elected as Colonel with the pro-confederacy Missouri State Guard in July 1861. He was with his soldiers in a cornfield above Wilson Creek when a battle with the Union soldiers from Springfield started.

George had not yet joined the Union, but when he heard about the battle at Wilson Creek, he rode his horse to the battle. Robert and George met on the battlefield that day. George was injured and was sent to the hospital in Springfield. He died on October 9, 1861, not from his injuries, but instead from typhoid fever. He was forty-nine years old and was buried next to his son, Little Clarence, in the family cemetery. His wife, Mary Ann, was left with seven children to raise on her own.

After losing everything he had, Robert returned to Mount Vernon after the war and continued his law practice. He collapsed while in court and died October 19, 1873, at age sixty-one. He was buried near his stepbrother George Catts at the family cemetery.

After ten years of traveling on the Oregon Trail and feeling responsible to take care of his mother after his stepfather died, Thomas L. Catts died at age sixty-three, on April 23, 1880. He was buried next to his brother, George Catts, in the family cemetery. Jane Ann Catts Crawford, his sister, died September 6, 1888, at age seventy-five, and was buried in the family cemetery beside her husband Robert.

At the white farm house on the Catts/Crawford farm, Frances Neal Catts Crawford died on April 24, 1890, at age ninety-eight years old. She was buried beside her son, Thomas L. Catts, and near her son Robert in the Catts/Crawford Cemetery in the hayfield. Frances lost two husbands and outlived all of her children. She was married for only seventeen years and widowed for over fifty-two years. She cared for her family on her own for almost sixty-five years.

Mary Ann Catts, a widow for almost fifty years, died July 19, 1910, at age eighty-nine. She was buried beside the love of her life, George Catts.

Fannie Catts died on a cold day, December 7, 1910, at age seventy. She was buried beside her mother in the family cemetery. She was the last person buried in the family cemetery in the hayfield.

The seven gravestones mark where each was buried, but a gravestone has never been found for Little Clarence Catts.

Tate, Pops, and Grams sat staring at one another in silence. "What an amazing family we've found," Grams said. Tired, they went off to bed.

The next morning, Pops and Grams were so tired, they stayed in bed a bit longer than normal. Suddenly, there came a pounding on their bedroom door.

"There is one more key! I have one more key!" Tate yelled, gasping for breath.

Their feet hit the floor immediately. They got dressed and met Tate at the stairway door. Without having breakfast, they raced to the top of the wooden steps, each darting into a different bedroom. They search everything that was in each room but could find nothing that had a lock.

Pops went back into the attic to search the corners with a flashlight while Tate and Grams searched each room again.

Grams walked over to an old, tall, tiger-oak dresser with swirls of carving across the top of an oval mirror and across the bottom.

"This looks pretty old," Tate said.

"Yeah," Pops replied. "The bureau was left in the house when my parents bought the farm almost seventy-five years ago. No one ever said why it was left behind, but everyone always assumed it was just too heavy to carry down the steps."

In the center of the dresser were two drawers with a door on each side. Grams told them that was where ladies used to store their hats. Underneath were three wide drawers across the front.

"I cleaned each drawer when Pops and I moved in and used the drawers to store keepsakes that had belonged to Pops' parents."

Pulling open the wide drawers first, she and Tate searched to the bottom of each drawer for anything that might have a lock. Then they searched the two small drawers in the center, but they found nothing.

Grams pulled open the door on the left side of the small drawers. She found small hats and gloves and purses.

Grams had her head down, busy sorting the items she found in the other door.

Pops walked into the room, shaking his head. "I didn't find anything with a lock in the attic."

Tate pulled on the door of the dresser. "It won't open."

"Oh, we never found a key for it," Grams replied, concentrating on what she was sorting.

At the same moment, all three looked up into the oval dresser mirror. Time stopped as they stared at one another.

Tate broke out in a huge smile on his round freckled face as he removed the seven keys from his pocket. He had one last unused key—a small skeleton key.

He inserted the key into the brass key hole on the dresser door and turned it. He pulled on the handle. The door opened.

Not moving or saying a word, they all three stared at a stack of books neatly placed inside the door. Lying on top was a brown leather book tied with thin strips of leather.

As the east morning sun came shining through the window, Tate saw the word *Journal* cut into in the leather. Across the

bottom, embossed in gold, was the name *Frances*.

Looking at Grams and then at Pops, Tate picked up the journal. As he held the book in his hands, they stared at it, each with a shocked look on their faces.

Tate held his breath for a moment. Could this really be the journal of Frances Neal Catts Crawford?

Grams picked up the other books, and without talking, they all went down the wooden steps to the kitchen. Pulling out chairs at the breakfast table, they sat down.

Tate picked up the books one at a time and read the titles. The first was *Pilgrim's Progress*. Another was a book of poems by Shakespeare, and the third was a songbook. Laying them aside, Tate picked up the journal.

"I'll make us some breakfast," Grams announced.

"And I need my morning coffee," Pops said. "Strong coffee."

Tate rubbed the cover with his hand, still wondering why no one had ever found it.

Pops broke his concentration by saying, "Now, you will really know the story of Frances Neal Catts Crawford's life. She wrote in her journal, and someone hid the book for you to find, Tate."

"But why?" he asked softly.

Thinking about what Pops said, Tate untied the leather strips and turned the cover to open the journal. On the first page was written:

> *To our beloved daughter,*
> *Frances Neal*
> *Happy Seventh Birthday*
> *Our Love To You Always*
> *Mama and Papa*
> *February 8, 1799*
> *Never forget, God saved you for a special purpose.*

Not knowing what to say, Tate turned the next page and read, "My name is Frances Neal. Today I am seven. It is snowing. Mama made me a cake and this journal is my present. I will write the story of my life."

"It really is her. It's Frances's journal," Tate murmured in a soft voice.

PART II

CHAPTER 4

February 8, 1799
My name is Frances Neal. Today I am seven. It is snowing.
Mama made me a cake and this journal is my present. I will write
the story of my life.

February 14, 1799
Today is Valentine's Day. I made a pretty card for Mama and
Papa. I made a paper fan for my sister Rachel and a paper book for
brother John to write his poems in. We all found cookies under our
pillow from Mama.

February 14, 1799

An old family story was told of Frances's grandmother being related to Martha Washington's mother. It was never documented, only a story passed down through the family.

On their way to Philadelphia, President George Washington and Martha often stopped at the Neal house to visit. Perhaps it was a convenient stopping place to warm themselves on a cold day or a place to sit by the fire while they visited family.

Hearing a carriage pull up in front of their house and seeing who the passengers were, the Neal family welcomed them at the door. Assuming them to be tired from travel, they scurried to make them comfortable and to provide a warm meal.

Frances's father served under the command of Washington during the War of Independence. The President and he sat by the fire where they discussed the disturbing aggravations by the British Navy.

Martha Washington looked at new hat designs created by Frances's mother.

Frances read a poem to her that John, her brother, had written while Rachel wrapped Valentine cookies for them to take on their journey.

John warmed their coats and blankets near the fire and heated bricks to put under their feet to keep them warm on their carriage ride on to Philadelphia.

> *July 4, 1799*
> *Mama made blackberry cobbler for our picnic, and Papa wore his uniform in the parade. The colorful fireworks excited us all. The loud noise scared me, but I did not cry. I covered my ears and kept watching.*

July 4, 1799

For the twenty-third time, America celebrated our independence from the British. Governed by our own laws and by our own people, we are the United States of America. Thankful to God, celebrations were held in every city and community.

George Washington said, "It is the duty of all nations to acknowledge the providence of Almighty God, to obey His will, to be grateful for His benefits, and humbly to implore His protection and favor."

> *December 31, 1799 (Age 7 1/2)*
> *I liked to see the pretty colors of the fireworks. I wrapped up in a warm blanket to sit on Papa's lap while we watched from our balcony. Everyone was celebrating, and church bells were ringing.*

December 31, 1799

In a split second of time, the Eighteenth Century ended, and the Nineteenth Century began. The past and the future were only a moment apart.

Families lined the balconies of their row houses and filled the streets of Baltimore.

Loud, booming sounds scared some and excited others. The silence between booms was almost as stark as the noise had been.

Suddenly, radiant colors burst open in the dark night sky as fireworks exploded above the city. With each one, people cheered as they welcomed the future and said their goodbyes to the past.

So much had happened in the previous twenty-five years to write the history of the newly established United States of America. Thirteen colonies that sought their independence from Great Britain's control became a nation of their own.

The fast-growing United States inaugurated their second president, John Adams in 1797. Thomas Jefferson served as his Vice President.

On December 31, 1799, church bells rang as a new nation celebrated their past and looked forward to a bright future.

Only days before the end of the Eighteenth Century, "the Father of Our Nation," George Washington, passed away on December 14, 1799. The nation mourned the death of their beloved leader and founding father.

> *January 1, 1802 (Age 10)*
>
> *It was cold, and snow had started to fall. Mama made me a pretty new dress and matching coat to wear to Frankie's wedding to Ms. Polly. First, he danced with Ms. Polly. Then he danced with me. He swirled me around the room while I giggled. When we went outside in the cold to tell Frankie and Ms. Polly goodbye, I sneezed. He got down from their carriage, gave me his handkerchief and a hug goodbye. He promised we would be friends forever and always.*

January 1, 1802

The family of Francis Scott Key and the Neal family had been friends for many years. Baltimore was home for the Neals, and the Key family lived not far away at their Terra Rubra estate. When the families would get together, Frankie, as Francis Scott Key was called, would entertain the younger children.

His favorite bothersome little friend was Frances Neal. He was thirteen years her senior, so she looked up to Frankie as an older brother.

When she had yellow fever at age two, he was fifteen. Perhaps, through his prayers for her, they became spiritually connected for life. Anytime he traveled to Baltimore, he visited the Neal family to check on Frances. He would often read poetry to her.

When he got engaged to Mary Taylor Lloyd, he brought her to meet Frances. They too became friends. At their wedding, Frances watched as he first danced with his bride, Ms. Polly, as most people called her. Then he came over to ten-year-old Frances Neal, bowed, and asked her to dance.

They remained lifelong friends.

July 4, 1808 (Age 16)
Today I met the man I will marry. I bumped head-on into him at the Independence Day parade. He later came to sit with me at the picnic. He is handsome and bold in his faith and his political views. His big blue eyes sparkled when he smiled at me. I think I am in love. No, I know I am in love.

July 4, 1808

John William Catts, the man Frances fell in love with, was the son of patriot soldier, Michael Catts, who served his country in the Revolutionary War. Born July 8, 1787, in Baltimore, he was taught that everyone was expected to serve and defend America. So he volunteered to serve as a soldier.

All Americans showed great respect for the American flag and the meaning behind the colors. Red was for courage, hardness, and valor. White was for the purity, innocence, and peace of our nation. And blue signified vigilance, perseverance, and justice for all.

He met Frances Neal on July 4, 1808. He later wrote, "Today, I have fallen love."

July 4, 1810 (Age 18)

Today I will marry the man I love, John Catts. He is strong in his faith and will be a good father to our children. When I look into his big blue eyes, I see everything I will need in my future: his love, his devotion and his unwavering example of goodness. Mama has sewn me a beautiful wedding dress and veil. Knowing how devoted John is to our country, underneath my petticoat she has sewn a small red, white, and blue bow. Papa will pray over us at our wedding, our pastor will officiate the ceremony, and Mama will cry. I, however, will overflow with joy.

July 4, 1810

An undertone of talk of war with the British prevailed everywhere. The United States ports had reopened to all ships from other nations except to the French and the British. And no imports would be allowed from the two outcasts at all. The continuing irritation of the British may soon bring America back to war.

For the hearts of John Catts and Frances Neal, it was a perfect day to celebration their love. They would be married at noon on Independence Day.

Francis Scott Key and his wife, Ms. Polly, would attend the wedding before returning to Georgetown to watch the fireworks in Washington.

December 24, 1810

It is our first Christmas as husband and wife. Our tree is decorated and sits next to the warm fire, waiting for John to come home. My gift to him is a new shirt and coat that I have sewn for him. I hope he is pleased with the color. Two cakes sit on the table waiting to be taken to our family gatherings tomorrow. Tonight, we will have oyster stew, warm bread, and cookies for our Christmas Eve supper. Then we will walk in the snow to the candlelight service at the Old

Otterbein Church. John and I will pray together that God will soon bless us with children.

December 24, 1810

The church bells rang as friends and family entered the Old Otterbein Church in Baltimore for the Christmas Eve candlelight service. The bells were a call to one and all to come and celebrate the birth of Jesus. Carriages rolled through the snow-covered streets to bring families seeking to celebrate the true reason for the season.

Children reached up to catch one more snowflake before going inside to light their candles and to sing, "Hark the Herald Angels Sing." The sweet, spicy smells of cinnamon, nutmeg, and vanilla filled the air and welcomed family and friends home for Christmas.

Carolers stood at the street corners, singing and collecting money to feed the poor. 'Twas the season for everyone to be jolly.

John Catts had wrapped a special surprise for Frances in brown butcher paper and had tied it with a red ribbon. She'd so admired a white lace shawl in the mercantile window for months.

Through the lighted windows throughout the city of Baltimore, families could be seen celebrating Christmas together.

But the talk of war continued to be whispered.

July 4, 1811 (Age 19)

Today, John and I will celebrate our first anniversary. It is Independence Day, and all of America will celebrate with parades, picnics, and fireworks. John will be most surprised with my gift to him. I will tell him we are expecting our first child.

July 4, 1811

Everyone could feel the excitement of Independence Day. People waved flags as the parade marched through the city. Children's faces had crumbs of apple pie and their chins dripped with watermelon. People anxiously waited for fireworks to light up the deep blue night skies over Baltimore.

And huddled together around town were men still whispering about war.

> *December 20, 1811*
>
> *John heard that a terrible earthquake has hit to the west, in Missouri. The earth continues to shake, and some say that the worst is yet to come. I pray for the earthquake to stop and people to be safe. I also pray that I will never have need to visit or live in Missouri.*

December 16, 1811

A shocking earthquake shook southeast Missouri at 8:15 a.m. on the morning of December 16, registering between 7.5 and 7.9, and could be felt in a rippling effect for hundreds of miles around. Huge trees toppled, rivers and streams rolled with waves like a terrible storm, and wild animals could be heard screaming for help. Neither nature nor man could conceive what was happening.

Church bells rang in Baltimore and Boston, and windows rattled in Washington, DC.

More aftershocks would continue.

On January 23, 1812, the earth began to crack, rise, and split apart. Landslides occurred along the Mississippi River, and stream banks were carved away. More aftershocks continued.

February 7, an even worse earthquake hit the region, registering perhaps as high as 8.0. Chimneys crumpled in Saint Louis and Kansas City. The powerful and mighty Mississippi

River flowed backward for several days. New lakes were formed by the upheaving force of the earth and transformation of rivers. Property damage was severe, and many lives were lost.

Many thought it was the anger of God. Others thought it was the cracking and spewing of the earth from within.

To this day people wait for the next earthquake.

> *February 13, 1812*
> *John paced anxiously outside our bedroom door, waiting. The long-awaited sound of a baby crying began to echo in our house. Our son, George Neal Catts, was born. His little head is covered with dark hair, and his eyes are blue for now. John is beside himself as a new Papa. I am tired and sleepy but oh so excited to hold our new son in my arms. Thank you, God. May our son always serve you.*

February 13, 1812

On a cold day wintery day in Baltimore, a son, George Neal Catts, was born into the Catts family. He was named George, after President George Washington, and Neal, which was Frances's maiden name. His father, John Catts, could not have been prouder to have a new son to carry on his name. Life was good for the young family.

But dark clouds of war were again forming over the country. The whispers of war continued. Secret meetings were being held in surrounding communities. In Washington, DC, leaders were meeting to discuss declaring war with the British. Their talk was no longer whispers, but a loud, bold reality.

CHAPTER 5

June 12, 1812

I see groups of people gathering on the street corners. From the window I can hear them saying that war had been declared against the British. I hold baby George close as he nurses. What will his future be? Will we continue to be America or again be ruled by the British? John has already signed up to be a soldier. I pray the war will be swift and soon over.

June 12, 1812

America could no longer tolerate their ships being seized by the British and the capturing of US sailors to serve in the British Navy. The British were already knee-deep in war with France, but their annoying interference to stop American trade had to end.

The Senate and the House of Representatives voted to declare war against Great Britain. President James Madison signed the declaration of war on June 12, 1812.

In the heat of a hot, humid summer day, the war started on June 18th, and would last two long years and eight months.

February 14, 1813

I now know that I am expecting our second child. On my Valentine's Day card to John, I have signed it, "Our love always, Frances, George, and _____." I know he will be surprised, and that he is hoping for a baby girl to name after his mother. I too hope for a baby girl and a little sister for George.

February 14, 1813

Most families had no idea what was happening. Battles continued with the British up and down the east coast and in the Canadian Territory. Thirty to sixty Americans had been killed only weeks before in the River Raisin Massacre. Shocked by the massacre, Americans started a rally cry, "Remember the Raisin!" which was used to motivate soldiers until the end of the war.

July 8, 1813

Little George is now walking, or perhaps running is a better word. I am rounding outward as our baby grows. Mama always said that if you round out in front, it is a girl. I hope so, but I only ask that God bless us with a healthy, happy baby. Today is John's birthday. I am sad he is away on his birthday, so I will pray God will bless him in some special way today, wherever he is. Many people know that I make hats to help bring in money while John is away at war. A lady named Mrs. Pickersgill sent a note requesting to buy heavy white thread if I might have any. My sister Rachael came to watch George while I delivered the thread and some homemade sweet bread to her.

When I arrived at the address she gave me, I was surprised to find a brewery for beer. Entering, I saw the most amazing sight. Laying full length on the malt floor of the brewery was the largest flag I had ever seen.

Introducing myself to Mrs. Pickersgill and her daughter, Caroline, I handed her the thread she requested and a basket of sweet bread. She looked very tired, so I suggested she rest and enjoy the bread. She explained that she was behind in sewing since she ran out of thread.

While she rested, I threaded a needle, got on my knees, and began to sew on the huge strips of the flag. Seeing I was expecting, she was concerned. I assured her I was fine and continued to sew. We visited while I sewed the right bottom corner of the flag.

Rested and revived, she thanked me for the bread and tried to pay me for the thread. I refused, telling her that today was John's birthday and that he was a soldier in the war against the British. I was honored to give her the thread. I returned home, still amazed by the size of the flag.

July 8, 1813

In early summer, Major George Armistead, the commander of the fort that guards the Chesapeake Bay from British attacks, asked the widowed Mrs. Mary Pickersgill to sew a large flag to fly at Fort McHenry. Named after James McHenry, America's second Secretary of War, the star-shaped fort was built to defend the bay and the city of Baltimore. Major Armistead wanted a flag big enough for the British Navy to see for miles away.

He requested two flags be sewn. He wanted one as a storm flag, seventeen-by-twenty-five feet in size, and the second to be thirty-by-forty-two feet in size as their garrison flag.

Accepting the commission, Mrs. Pickersgill, her daughter, Caroline, her mother, her two nieces, and a free African American apprentice, Grace Wisher, began sewing. Four-hundred yards of English wool bunting fabric was used to make the large flags with fifteen stripes and fifteen stars—one for each of the fifteen states of the union. Each strip of red and white was to be two-feet wide and each bright-white cotton star was to be two feet, tip to tip. Weighing fifty pounds when completed, the flag was delivered to Fort McHenry on August 19, 1813.

Frances had no idea the flag she sewed on for a short time would be the flag her beloved friend, Francis Scott Key, would see as the dawn broke after the battle of Fort McHenry. Nor did she know it would be known as "The Star-Spangled Banner Flag."

No one in the family knew where John Catts was on his twenty-sixth birthday. He was a soldier at war wherever he was needed.

October 17, 1813

I watch the fall leaves blow past my window while I am having labor pains. In between, I write in my journal to distract my mind from the intense pain of having a baby. Little George plays with his toys in the floor. I am thankful my sister Rachael is with me since John is still away at war. Contractions are getting stronger and closer together, I will finish writing later.

Six hours later:

> *My baby girl has arrived, and her name is Jane Ann. Named after John's mother, I hope she is as kind and good hearted as his mother. I have sent a note with one of the soldiers to let John know his daughter has arrived safe, and I am doing well with Rachael's help.*

October 17, 1813

America was winning more of the battles in the war with the British. But the battles kept American soldiers on the move. John Catts came home to see his family and to hold his baby girl, Jane Ann.

> *August 24, 1814*
>
> *John is home to rest. Fighting the British has been long and difficult. On this hot August day, people are gathering in the street below our row house. Some have said that the British have invaded Washington, D.C. With little George asleep in his bed and baby Jane Ann asleep in her crib, John and I rush to the rooftop terrace to see for ourselves. I will never forget the distant sight that made my soul grieve. Forty miles away we could see the orange glow of our nation's capital city being burned to the ground by the British. We could smell the smoldering smoke. In fear we knew, "The British are coming for Baltimore next."*

August 24, 1814

Marching unopposed, British General Robert Ross invaded Washington, DC, after the Battle of Bladensburg to torch America's capital city. The marching soldiers sounded like thunder entering the city late in the afternoon. President James Madison and his wife, Dolly, escaped the city before the invaders arrived.

General Ross and other British commanders walked into the deserted White House. They sat at the formal dining table and feasted on the dinner that the first lady had servants prepare to serve guests that evening. They drank the wine that was to be served, took whatever they wanted, and threw fire torches through the windows, laughing as they turned to walk away. This was their revenge for the Americans burning the Canadian government buildings.

The White House, federal buildings, private homes, Capitol, House of Representatives, and Library of Congress were all set ablaze by the British soldiers. A torrential downpour of rain from an offshore hurricane storm and a tornado collided over DC. It turned the blazing fires into smoldering wet ashes. Many thought it was God's anger against the British.

Proud to have humiliated America by their vile invasion and destruction of America's capital city, the British celebrated. They thought the Chesapeake Bay port city of Baltimore would be their next easy victory.

September 7, 1814
  A soldier delivered a note addressed to me, saying Frankie had volunteered to board a British ship. He requested our prayers.

September 7, 1814

Distinguished Washington, DC, attorney Francis Scott Key had volunteered to go with a white flag of truce aboard a British ship and negotiate for the release of American prisoners. His negotiations were successful, but the British commanders realized that Key had heard their plans to attack Baltimore. He was not allowed to return to Baltimore but instead would have to watch his homeland attacked from a British ship.

September 13, 1814
  I wait and I listen. I hear many explosions and then silence, then more explosions. It has gone on for hours with no word from the Fort. Two flickering lanterns dimly light the basement of the Old Otterbein Church where I am taking refuge with my children and other families. It has rained most of the night. I hear the echoing

sound of dripping water in the cold basement. My beloved John is at Fort McHenry with other soldiers in the heat of the British attack. I did not tell him the news that I am expecting another baby.

My treasured friend, Francis Scott Key, is being held aboard a British ship. Word came after midnight that our soldiers at North Point were taking heavy casualties. I pray my brother, John, and family friend, Thomas Crawford, are safe. I pull little George close as baby Jane Ann whimpers in my arms. I feel her warmth against the tiny baby in my womb. Again, there is silence.

I feel my heart pounding. I can contain myself no more. I call out to God. I pray out loud as others joined in.

Our Father, who art in heaven,
hallowed be thy Name.
Thy kingdom come, thy will be done
on earth as it is in heaven.
Give us this day our daily bread.
And forgive us our trespasses,
as we forgive those
who trespass against us.
And lead us not into temptation,
but deliver us from evil.
For thine is the kingdom,
and the power, and the glory,
for ever and ever. Amen.

The bombardment of Fort McHenry, Maryland, September 13, 1814

The moment Frances Neal Catts began to pray the Lord's Prayer, twelve thousand soldiers and volunteers defending Baltimore on the east, one thousand soldiers at Fort McHenry, Francis Scott Key with other prisoners held on a British ship, twelve hundred men on small boats, and countless others all looked toward heaven. Unknowingly, at the exact same moment, they all called out to God for help. "Our Father ..."

Their prayers must have sounded like a roar of thunder calling out to God. And he answered.

An Impossible Battle For America To Win.

The largest navy in the world set their sights on the vital port city of Baltimore for their next decisive victory. They openly advanced their way up the Chesapeake Bay to prepare for the attack. Assuming victory would be swift, and that a British flag would be flying over Fort McHenry before sunrise, ships took their position in the shallow waters near Baltimore. Five bomb boats, ten warships, and a rocket vessel all pointed weapons at the American flag flying over the star-shaped fort.

North of Baltimore four thousand, five hundred British troops landed the day before on the tip of North Point, armed and ready to quickly seize what they assumed to be the unprepared city of Baltimore. Confident their enemy would surrender when they saw the massive number of forces, they moved inland.

Instead, they encountered well-armed American patriots and volunteers. Heavy rain slowed down the soldiers, so they elected to remain outside of Baltimore through the night. Early the next morning the British advanced their forces along the Philadelphia Road toward Baltimore.

Here the British encountered twelve thousand Americans behind built-up earthworks, ready to defend their families, their city, and their country. Unable to find a weakness in the American blockade or to overcome the Americans, the British held their position to wait for the naval attack to weaken the defense of the city.

British Admiral Alexander Cochrane, the commander of the Royal Navy's ships, moved his fleet up the Patapsco River closer to the fort. He prepared to take aim at the American flag.

Under the command of Major George Armistead, one thousand Americans at Fort McHenry came under fire by the British Navy at six thirty a.m., with heavy mortar shell bombs and Congreve rockets.

The brave Americans intensified fire at the ships with guns and cannons, forcing the ships to pull back. The British tried to move to the other side of the fort but were met by twelve hundred men waiting in boats. After taking heavy crossfire resulting in heavy losses, the largest navy in the world withdrew from the Chesapeake waters, and the ground forces retreated to North Point where they returned to British ships.

In an almost disastrous moment, a British shell struck the ammunition supply inside the fort. Hailed as the protection of God, the shell did not explode.

During the attack, four Americans were killed and twenty-four were wounded. John Catts, husband of Frances Neal Catts, received shrapnel wounds.

CHAPTER 6

The unsuccessful twenty-five-hour bombardment of Baltimore ended. The British suffered hundreds of losses and had fired over fifteen hundred bombs and rockets at Fort McHenry with little impact.

The rain stopped before dawn. The smaller American storm flag, ragged and torn from the battle, was lowered. The garrison flag was raised at daybreak. Waving over Fort McHenry was the thirty-foot-high by forty-two-foot-long American flag. The proud banner was the last thing the British Navy saw as they backed their ships away from the United States of America in defeat.

With a gentle breeze, the dawn's early light broke the darkness. Attorney Francis Scott Key, who was being held by the British, looked through his telescope just as the smoke cleared. He was deeply touched by what he saw. The huge American flag still flew over Fort McHenry.

Welling up with a thankful heart at the sight of the flag, Key took paper from his pocket and wrote a poem describing what he saw as he looked toward the fort. He was later released by the British to go back to Baltimore.

Major George Armistead's men celebrated with cheers when their lookout announced the ships were leaving the harbor. Americans came back to Baltimore to celebrate the victory over the British. Children helped ring the bells at Old Otterbein Church to announce the battle was won.

Those who called on God in their hour of need before the battle for Baltimore praised God for the victory of the impossible battle for America to win.

Although said at a different time and place, these words were true of our nation in the past, the present, and hopefully, in our future.

September 14-16, 1814

I am deeply thankful to God that the soldiers brought John home so I can care for his wounds. Although he is injured, he is home with us. I lay cool cloths on his wounds as he moans in pain while he sleeps. Little George cries for his Papa, but he must wait until he is stronger. The soldiers said the British ships are quickly retreating from the bay in defeat.

They also heard that the lawyer, Francis Scott Key, and the prisoners have been released from the British ship. I inquired where might he be, and we were told he is in a room above the tavern resting. I quickly had a note delivered to him, letting him know John had been injured. He soon came to pray at John's bedside.

While John slept, Frankie and I took a walk in our rose garden. He read me the poem he wrote when he saw the flag still standing above the fort. He told me that the words overflowed from his heart as praise to God for His protection.

Although tired, Frankie rode by horseback home to his family. I went back to sit with John while Rachael took care of little George and baby Jane Ann.

I got on my knees beside John's bed and thanked God for hearing our prayers from the basement of the old Otterbein Church.

September 14-16, 1814

In total defeat, the British backed their massive ships out of the Chesapeake Bay. They released the prisoners and Francis Scott Key as their last act of kindness to the Americans. Key returned to Baltimore to rest in a hotel room above a local tavern. He finished the poem he had written when he saw the American flag still flying above the fort.

Although exhausted, when he heard that his friend John Catts had been injured during the battle, he immediately went to their home. After praying with John, he and his dear friend Frances took a walk in the rose garden where he read his poem to her that he titled, "Defense of Fort McHenry." He had the well-known pub song, "To Anacreon in Heaven," flowing through his mind when he wrote the poem. In the fourth verse, as a lawyer, he made his closing statement after watching America win the impossible battle. He wrote, "Let this be our motto, In God is our trust." Frances Catts held on to the last five words from his poem for the rest of her life.

Key's brother-in-law took the poem to a Baltimore paper. They printed the verse with a new title, "The Star-Spangled Banner." The poem spread like wild fire in papers across the country. Put to the tune Key had in mind, soon the song was sung all around the country.

Always a humble man of deep faith, Key never claimed fame from the song. He first praised God, and then he honored every person who served under the American flag.

Frances Catts clung to Key's motto. She wrote his words in the front of their family Bible.

During the long months of healing from his wounds, John Catts carved the words "In God is our trust" on a board to hang on their mantel. He gave it to Frances for Christmas.

December 24, 1814

We will stay at home tonight for Christmas Eve. John has not healed from his shrapnel wounds. And I am expecting another gift, a new baby in spring. We watch from our window as the snow falls, and we listen to the beautiful sound of the church bells calling families to come and celebrate the birth of Jesus. We will be happy at home as long as we are together.

As a very special surprise for John, I sent a note to Major Armistead's wife, asking if I may have a piece of the flag that John fought under at Fort McHenry. I explained his wounds still have not healed, and I would like to give it to him as a

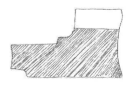

Christmas gift. She cut off the right bottom corner of the flag and had it delivered to me. I am so very grateful to her. She does not know that is the piece of the flag that I sewed while Mrs. Pinkergill rested.

My brother, John Neal, made a special wooden box to hold the treasured piece of the flag. I have it wrapped, waiting for John to open tomorrow on Christmas morning. I know he will show our children it is the flag he and others fought under to assure their future freedom.

December 24, 1814

The Treaty of Ghent was signed that ended the War of 1812 between the United States and Great Britain. The impossible battle, won by the protection of God, was not easily forgotten. Plans were immediately made to rebuild the capital city of Washington, DC, and to strengthen their military force.

Americans sang Francis Scott Key's poem and echoed his closing statement, "In God is our trust."

Commander Armistead was presented the flag after the battle at Fort McHenry. He placed his wife in charge of it. Many families wrote to Mrs. Armistead requesting a piece of the flag. Knowing how important it was to them, she cut off many pieces. The Star-Spangled Banner Flag became part of the Smithsonian Collection in Washington, DC, and is permanently displayed at the American History Museum. Originally thirty-feet by forty-two feet in size, the flag is minus eight feet. Mrs. Armistead cut away piece by piece to honor patriot soldiers. One star is missing that is assumed to have been buried with Commander Armistead. Only seven pieces have ever been recovered from the flag.

February 14, 1815
Today I will count my blessings. Although John's wounds continue to give him pain, he is home with our children. On the days he feels good, he works with his uncle in his law office. Little George is a

strong-willed three-year-old. Jane Ann's sweet smile reminds John of his mother who passed away while staying with us during the winter. I feel good and am excited to greet our new baby soon. I am thankful to be strong as I care for our family. And I am grateful I can sew and make hats to help make money for our family. In God is my trust.

February 14, 1815

Early purple crocus pushed their way up on a warm February day. White snowdrop flowers were a reminder that perhaps we still might have snow, but at that time, they were a beautiful glimpse of spring. People were thankful the war had ended. Fathers had returned home to their families. Farmers anxiously waited for the soil to warm so they could plant their crops. Children waited for warm days to play kick-the-can on the side streets of Baltimore. Mothers would soon open their windows to let fresh air and sunshine into their homes. The promise of spring was a sign of hope to all, a new hope in everyone's heart.

May 23, 1815
I am exhausted but oh so happy. After long hours of hard labor, our son, John Neal Catts, was born today. Named after my brother, John Neal, he is a rosy-cheeked healthy baby boy. My husband, John, is happy to have another son. George wants to hold his brother. Jane Ann just wants to touch him as she giggles. They are all asleep, even baby John Neal. I will rest for a while.

May 23, 1815

John Catts happily welcomed his new son, John Neal. Still only working part time, John struggled to provide for his growing family. Perhaps the battle for Baltimore gave the community a special bonding. Fear before the battle and thankful hearts afterward opened their hearts to care for one another. So many neighbors and friends helped each another through difficult times as though they were family.

Francis Scott Key and Polly brought baskets of food for the Catts family each time they came to Baltimore. All prayed for John's healing from his wounds.

> *July 4, 1815*
> *I am up early cooking food for our Fourth of July Independence Day family picnic. John is in so much pain, so we will have our picnic on the terrace on the roof. I have made soap bubbles for the children to blow and John's favorite blackberry cobbler with cream. We will have our own private picnic and will be thankful we are together.*

July 4, 1815

This was a special Independence Day, especially for the people in Baltimore—their first Fourth of July celebration since the battle for Baltimore. For the Neal family, John's painful injuries were a constant reminder that freedom wasn't free but instead, came with a price to many families. For him, this reminder was his wounds that wouldn't heal. For others less fortunate, it was a life freely given to pay the price for others.

> *July 8, 1816*
> *John is feeling good today. I baked a triple-layered chocolate cake for his twenty-ninth birthday. Little George does his best to sing Happy Birthday to his Papa. He has been singing it all day. Sweet Jane Ann has given her Papa hugs and kisses all day. Tiny John Neal crawled to his Papa and wanted up on his lap. John has smiled all day, and that makes me happy.*

July 8, 1816

Two months earlier, the American Bible Society was established, which began as the United States nondenominational Bible society which published and translated the Bible. They also provided pocket Bibles to all soldiers during the Civil War. Francis Scott Key served as vice president of the society for over twenty-five years. The first translation by the American Bible Society in 1818 was to a Native American language.

The Delphian Club was established in 1816 in Baltimore—the first club for professional writers and poets. Thought to have allowed only nine members at a time, Francis Scott Key and John Neal, Frances Catt's brother, were members at the same time.

> *December 24, 1816*
>
> *The children are asleep. John and I sat by the fire tonight, hypnotized by the waltzing orange and yellow flames. Snow, still falling, piled in the corners of the windows and on the ledge. Our little Christmas tree has the packages for the children tucked underneath. John will not spend money on himself, so I bought him a much-needed pair of new shoes. Mr. Paul said I can exchange them if another size is needed. John refuses to talk about his wounds. They still have not healed. We will be thankful for each day God gives us together, especially Christmas Day.*

December 24, 1816

In 1798, former President George Washington described Baltimore as the "risingest town in America." The Federal Government began building the National Road from the Ohio River to Cumberland, Maryland. A group of businessmen paid to have the road finished all the way to Baltimore. This became a road "much traveled," as a lifeline to the Ohio valley. Imports and exports grew by leaps and bounds.

Baltimore was considered the largest city in America and became a city for education and culture. The first purpose-built museum opened in Baltimore. The Peale Museum exhibited paintings, sculptures, and the bones of a mastodon. Libraries and literary clubs were established to compliment education. Baltimore was the place to be in 1816.

April 6, 1817

Today is a beautiful Easter Sunday morning. I got up early to make breakfast for John. As I opened the tall windows in the hearth room, I heard the church bells ringing, calling us to come and worship our risen Savior. From our window I can see red and yellow tulips in bloom in the gardens across the street. Perhaps the cool fresh morning breeze will make John feel better. I know he will smile when I tell him I am expecting a new baby. I hear the children stirring, so my quiet moment is finished for now.

April 6, 1817

John Catts was not gaining but losing strength. With three children, another on the way, and John requiring more care, Frances needed help. She asked her unmarried sister Rachael to move into their home. She could help with the children while Frances did sewing and hat making. Since John no longer worked part time, Frances needed to make and sell more hats. She was developing quite the following of locals wanting her custom hat designs. But her heart's desire was to first care for John.

December 6, 1817

Childbirth is so painful. If it weren't for the beautiful prize I receive from my labor, I don't think I could stand it. Mama told me before George was born that when I see my new baby for the first time, I would not remember the pain. Mama was right. This morning I gave birth to another strong baby boy. John would like to name him Thomas, after Thomas Jefferson. His middle name will be Love, as a tribute to me for giving birth to our four children. George, now five, almost six, sees baby Thomas as a new playmate. Jane Ann, now over four, would like to play with Thomas like a dress-up doll. Little John Neal is two and a half. He wants to snuggle with Thomas as a cuddly teddy bear. I just want to hold all my babies close.

I can see John's strength slipping away. The doctor said there is nothing more that can be done for him. As best I can, I will keep him comfortable and make his last Christmas with us his best.

December 6, 1817

Baltimore was experiencing an unusually cold winter. Frances Catts didn't even notice. Her aching heart was wearing her down. Although excited about her new son, Thomas L., and determined to seem happy to everyone around her, she knew she was spending her last days with her husband, John.

Frances's mother taught her when she was a little girl to get on her knees every night to say her prayers out loud to God. Each night she would begin praying, "I thank you, Heavenly Father, for another good day that has come and gone." As Frances watched her husband's condition weaken, she prayed beside his bed. But she found it more difficult to thank God for a "good day."

February 28, 1818

I was on my knees beside John's bed, holding his hand until he took his last breath. I could barely hear his voice as he told me one last time that he loved me and for me to never stop telling the children how much he loved them. His breathing stopped, and his pain ended.

Rachael and my brother, John, cared for the children while I sat with John for a long time. Remembering the day I met him when we fell in love, I smiled through my tears. Thinking about the many days we were so happy together and the days we cried happily when each of our children were born. I thought about how thankful I was to see his face when the soldiers brought him home from the fort injured from the battle but alive. Through his pain, he smiled when he saw me.

So many memories and so much love now lay silent. I held his hand and kissed his cheek once more before pulling the sheet over him. With tears I could not stop, I wondered how I could thank God for this being a "good day." I was thankful my faithful friends, Frankie and Ms. Polly, came to sit with me before John died.

February 28, 1818

The news of John Catts being in his last days traveled fast. When Francis Scott Key heard John was gravely ill, he and Ms. Polly left for Baltimore immediately. They sat beside John's bed and prayed for him through the night. Wanting to see John's smile once more, Francis Scott Key stood up beside the bed and began to softly sing the "Star-Spangled Banner."

Frances placed the piece of the Star-Spangled Banner flag in John's hand. He held tightly to her hand and to the piece of the flag.

Francis Scott Key continued, 'O! Say does that star-spangled banner yet wave, O'er the land of the free and the home of the brave?"

Respectfully with love, they left Frances with John for their last few moments together.

John Catts died at age thirty with his wife Frances at his side.

March 2, 1818

Today I laid my beloved John to rest. His pain has ended. George, Jane Ann, John Neal, and Thomas in my arms stood together. Frankie, Polly, my brother John, and Rachael helped me through the day. I know it was only God's loving hands that held my broken heart together.

I was humbled to see Lieutenant Colonel Armistead at John's funeral as well as so many soldiers he served with at the fort. The Colonel's eyes were filled with tears as he shook my hand, then he stepped back and saluted my children for their father's service to America.

It began to snow as we walked away from the grave. I noticed white snowdrop flowers peeking out at us from under the edge of a trellis. I thought perhaps that was God letting me know that his teardrops were falling with mine.

Only George will probably remember his father, but I will strive to keep his memory alive by telling them stories about their Papa.

*Again tonight, I will ask God to give me the strength to thank him
for this, another good day.*

March 2, 1818

Frances Catts was dressed in black as she mourned for her
husband, John Catts, her heart broken. Friends and family
stayed by her side during and after John passed away. He was
a respected and honored man. And he was deeply loved by his
family.

Sadly, Colonel Armistead passed away at the fort on April
25, 1818. He was honored by the soldiers who served with him.
Mrs. Armistead, still having control of the Star-Spangled Banner
flag, was thought to have removed one of the stars so it could be
buried with her husband.

CHAPTER 7

July 4, 1818

Today, John and I would have been married eight years. In four days, he would have been thirty-one years old. For reasons only God knows, he chose for us to be together for only a short time. I will choose to be thankful for the time God allowed us to be married and for the children he blessed us with. As I laid the flowers on his grave, I asked God to help me to always be thankful, even when my heart hurts so deeply.

In John's honor, today on our anniversary and in celebration of Independence Day, I will hang a sign on the front of our house that reads, "Catts Fine Millinery Shop."

Since we are close to other places of business and on Lexington Avenue, we will live in the back part of the house and have a hat shop in the front. My sister Rachael has remained with me to help me with the children and making hats. For her kindness, I am grateful. With God all things are possible—even a hat shop.

July 4, 1818

Baltimore continued to be a growing city and never forgot the battle impossible for them to win. They honored the soldiers who served and helped the families whose loved ones had passed away. From the day Frances hung her hat shop sign, she had the full support of the community. Ladies came from far and near to buy hats at the "Catts Fine Millinery Shop."

Frances was blessed and thankful to be able to support her family.

December 24, 1818

My first Christmas without John and my children's first Christmas without Papa. Exhausted from sewing, I cry myself to sleep each night. But I will do my best to make it a happy Christmas for the children. John had carved wooden toys for each of them before he passed away. They are wrapped and waiting under the tree. I too made some special gifts for them. I tell myself every day to be thankful and to always thank God for another good day, no matter how hard it might be.

I am blessed.

December 24, 1818

Frances missed John the most at Christmas. When she saw families celebrating the holidays together, she longed for her true love even more. But Frances Catts was a woman with true grit. She was determined with God's help to raise her family and to make new memories. On Christmas morning, snow covered the ground. There was a cold northeast wind blowing.

George and Jane Ann found a kite for them underneath the tree. Frances bundled them up, and they headed outside. While other families were warm inside and celebrating together, Frances was flying a kite with her children. Rachael held John Neal up in the window to watch while baby Thomas slept.

George and Jane Ann never forgot flying a kite on Christmas morning.

July 4, 1819

I go to sleep at night thinking of new hat designs, and I wake up thinking of new hat designs. The hat shop is closed today for Independence Day. Today is also my wedding anniversary. I miss John so much. I got up early to make a basket lunch for the Fourth of July picnic. We will attend the parade, go for the picnic, and watch the fireworks after dark. It will be a full day for the children and for my sister, but I know I must stay busy today.

July 4, 1819

The Catts Millinery Shop became well known in Baltimore. Ms. Polly encouraged ladies in her social circles to visit the shop, hoping to increase business for Frances. Frankie had Frances make two hats for him. He passed out cards for her shop to politicians and lawyers in Washington. The shop was keeping

Frances so busy, she needed to get away. On Independence Day, she spent the entire day with her children. They played kick-the-can on their way home. She felt good to be able to go outside and to turn her mind away from the hat shop, if only for one day.

December 24, 1819
The children are filled with excitement for Christmas morning. Tonight, we will go with another family to the Christmas candlelight service at the Old Otterbein Church. While John was sick, we were not able to attend but were always thankful to hear the bells ring before the service, a reminder for John to tell George and Jane Ann the story of Jesus's birth. I continued his tradition after the service. I have not placed the packages under the tree yet. I caught George peeking to see if he could find the gifts.

December 24, 1819

Excited to make something special for her children, Frances saved delicate laces and soft fabrics from the hat shop to make Jane Ann a Victorian doll. She worked for weeks finishing the details on the doll. She made George a monkey from tapestry fabric, and John Neal, a soft bear. Little Thomas will get a rabbit made of brown fur with embroidered eyes.

Frances made a new dress for her sister, Rachael, as a special thank you for all she did to help. And she made a new top hat for her brother, John. Looking at herself in the mirror, she could see she too needed a new dress. After the children were asleep in bed, she sat alone by the fire for a while looking at the Christmas gift John had carved for her—the sign that said, "In God is our trust."

She fell asleep with sweet memories of John.

February 13, 1820
George is turning eight years old today. I have taken the day off to spend with my children. It is cold, and a soft fluffy white snow

fell all during the night. We will start our day with a basket of cranberry scones. Then go outside to play in the snow. Sweet Jane Ann will lay in the cold snow to make snow angels. George will freeze his hands to build a huge snowman. He has already picked out the name Wilbur for his snowman. John Neal will roll snow balls for the battle he intends to win against his older brother. Rachael will bring little Thomas out for just a short while. I hope they will not forget this day.

February 13, 1820

The harbors are filled with ships from around the world. New businesses are coming to Baltimore, and the city is growing like never before. Ladies want more elaborate hats and gloves to match. Frances is thankful for the abundance of business but knows she needs more time with her children. Between homeschooling and the hat shop, she too needs a fun day.

October 17, 1820

Today Jane Ann is turning seven years old. Her birthday request is to spend the day with me in the hat shop and to make a new winter bonnet. I thought she was perhaps too young. But she proved me wrong. She had already envisioned her design and the fabric. It took most all day, but her bonnet was finished. She was so pleased, and I was so proud of her. When I checked her stitches to be sure they would hold, to my surprise, she seems to have a talent for sewing. As an extra surprise, I gave her a sewing basket. Just a small round brown one with a tassel and bead attached to the top. She was so excited. Nothing gives me greater joy than to see my children happy.

October 17, 1820

Hats, hats, and more hats! There were days when that was all Frances saw or heard about. Every lady in Baltimore seemed to want a hat from, "Catts Fine Millinery Shop." To think of making hats for the rest of her days was an unbearable thought for

Frances. However, on her daughter, Jane Ann's seventh birthday, she saw a possibility for a new generation of hat makers.

> *January 1, 1821*
>
> *I feel a new beginning. A new year filled with hope and new possibilities. I think I should travel this year with the children. They, as well as I, need to explore beyond Baltimore. Perhaps I will go to Washington to visit Frankie and Ms. Polly. I could go to Boston or New York where I have family. I have hired an experienced young hat maker. She will be wonderful to help in the shop when I need to be away. The children are waking up. They will find cookies under their pillows as my New Year's morning surprise.*

January 1, 1821

President James Monroe was to be sworn into office for his second term.

Emperor Napoleon died in exile on Saint Helena Island.

Missouri was admitted as the twenty-fourth state of the Union, and *The Saturday Evening Post* was published for the first time as a weekly newspaper.

Times were changing, and America was growing. The Santa Fe Trail was used for travel between Independence, Missouri, and Santa Fe, New Mexico. America was exploring the unknowns of the west.

> *May 23, 1821*
>
> *Not to my surprise, John Neal has asked for something special for his sixth birthday. He wants to spend the day with my brother whom he was named after, learning to write. He wants to learn from him the swirling script letters that he uses when he writes poetry. My brother is honored to teach his namesake what he loves most—writing. John has had many of his works published and is somewhat well known for his opinionated views on life. I went to the mercantile to purchase John Neal a new writing pad and pen as*

his gift. His birthday cake awaits him on the dining table. It is hard to imagine John Neal will have six candles to blow out.

May 23, 1821

John Neal, brother to Frances Neal Catts, was a self-educated, successful writer and poet. His work was published in periodicals, and he helped establish a literary society known as the Delphian Club where he wrote and edited the Delphian monthly journal. His family was friends with the Key family for many years. Francis Scott Key, now a well-known Washington attorney, encouraged John to attend law school while he continued his writing. He became a lawyer, a dry goods store owner, a boxer, and an architect. But his love was always writing.

> *February 8, 1822*
>
> *I am thirty years old today. I feel much older and I look much older. Raising four children on my own and keeping up with the demands of the millinery shop makes me feel so old at times. Rachael and her assistant will take care of the shop while I run away with my children to Washington, D.C., for four days. We will stay in a hotel, eat in restaurants, see how the city has been rebuilt and on Sunday, attend church with Frankie and Ms. Polly. Their children are excited to see my children and have a birthday surprise planned for me. Our bags are sitting by the door, my brother's carriage will soon await us, and for me this is an adventure I have long desired. We are on our way.*

February 8, 1822

The capitol city of Washington, DC, only forty miles from Baltimore, was a long trip in 1822. Frances Catts set out on her journey with four children, to celebrate her thirtieth birthday. She had not traveled since her husband, John, was injured during the battle at Fort McHenry. The weather was cold, but the sun was shining, and her brother John provided warm bricks in the carriage to keep their feet warm.

As they entered the city, the children strained to see all they could from their seat in the carriage. John didn't tell Frances their first stop would be the White House. Painted white in 1798 to protect the sandstone, the building was again painted white after being rebuilt in 1817. Perhaps, at that time, the white was to cover up the scorch marks caused by the fire set by the British in 1814. John had arranged for Frances and the children to tour the White House.

While walking down a long hall on their tour of the White House, President and Mrs. Monroe heard the children and stepped out to meet them.

On Sunday morning, they were welcomed by the entire Key family at church. Ms. Polly served a birthday lunch for Frances, and her surprise gift was a hand-written copy of "The Star-Spangled Banner" in a thin, gold-rubbed frame. On the front, the poem had been signed and dated by Frankie. On the back was written, "To Frances Neal Catts. Happiest blessed birthday. Our love always." Ms. Polly and all eleven Key children signed their names as well as Frances's children George, Jane Ann, John Neal, and Thomas. Her brother, John, and Francis Scott Key were the last to sign.

Frances later placed the frame on the hearth beside

In God Is Our Trust

the wooden box that contained the piece of the flag. Above the hearth was the sign, "In God is our trust," carved by her beloved John Catts.

April 1, 1823

My dearly loved younger brother, John Neal, announced to me today that he is going to London in late fall to live and to pursue his writing career. With bitter-sweet emotions, I am happy for him to follow his dream but oh so saddened for me and my children. He has filled the empty spot of a father in my children's lives. Each one has a deep connection to him. George has an interest to learn mercantile knowledge from him. Jane Ann is interested in accounting so she can own her own millinery shop someday. John Neal, his namesake, so much wants to learn to become a writer and follow in his footsteps. Young Thomas enjoys learning to fish. How sad our hearts will be to see him go, but he has promised to write us letters often to tell us about London.

Before leaving, he gave me our Papa's silver watch. As the oldest son, he would like for it to be given to George. For Jane Ann he left a journal, and for John Neal he left his best writing pen. Before leaving, he promised young Thomas to take him fishing for his early six-year-old birthday present. He will leave his fishing box for Thomas.

Our life will never be the same when he is gone.

April 1, 1823

John Neal published more than seventeen books and edited for many publications. Known for being a fast writer, John Neal once said, "I shall write as others drink—for exhilaration." When challenged, he completed a novel in one week. When his successful career was at a peak, he was often asked to critique another writer's and artist's work. John critiqued Edgar Allan Poe's writing and Benjamin Paul Akers's work as a sculptor.

John Neal was credited for discovering the art of Charles Codman, a noted American painter from Maine. Shortly thereafter, the Smithsonian American Art Museum added Codman's work to their permanent collection.

A health-conscience man, John was credited with starting gymnasiums for athletes throughout Maine. He was referred to as "The Father of Organized Maine Athletics." With a solid physique even in his old age, he displayed his strength at the age of seventy-nine by throwing a rude cigar-smoking man off a non-smoking street car.

October 6, 1823

I thought my brother John had forgotten his promise to young Thomas. It is two months before Thomas will be six years old, but he is very determined. Thomas has what he thinks is his fishing equipment sitting by the door ready to go. It has been there for at least a month. He is so excited to fish with his Uncle John. They will leave early to fish from the pier for flounder. It is early for winter flounder, but I hope he will catch at least one. It will give him his bragging rights to his older brothers. He has asked John a hundred times to tell him the difference between a black back flounder and a lemon sole flounder.

John laughs and tells him, "One is black, and the other is yellow."
For a six-year-old, this will be a memory he will never forget.

October 6, 1823

Thomas kept watching the clock move slowly. He waited by the door for his Uncle John to take him fishing. From the heart of a six-year-old whose Papa died not long after he was born, this would be a big adventure.

Uncle John arrived by carriage, and Thomas leapt from the stoop step into the carriage, and off they went.

While unloading the fishing box at the pier, Thomas didn't notice that under the hasp of the aged wooden box with metal handles, his Uncle John had carved the letters, T.L.C.

While showing Thomas how to bait his line and how to cast, Uncle John noticed he was a natural fisherman. They fished for only a short time before Thomas pulled in a lemon-sole flounder, then another and another. Tired from slinging his pole into the water, Uncle John suggested they rest for a while.

Talking while they rested, Uncle John took a silver compass from his pocket and laid it Thomas's hand. He told him he might need a compass in life.

Pulling the fishing box closer, he showed Thomas where he'd carved his initials on the front of the box. A million-dollar smile covered Thomas's round boyish face.

Captivated by his smile, Uncle John did a pencil drawing of Thomas, his fish, and his fishing box. Thomas kept the drawing, the fishing box, and the memory forever.

> *August 9, 1824*
>
> *Almost a year has passed since my brother John went to London. We have had four letters telling about his adventures. I read them repeatedly to the children. Thomas asks me to read them to him before he goes to bed at night as a reminder to pray for Uncle John.*
>
> *My young John Neal has been sick for the last two days. His fever is high, and he is very week. His skin is yellow in color. I pray with all my heart it is not Yellow Fever. Some people have said the ships from tropical islands are bringing mosquitos with them. Dearest God, please do not let John Neal have the fever. He seemed to feel a litter better after lunch, but now he is even weaker.*
>
> *Soon, the doctor came and has confirmed it is the fever. Although the other children are already exposed, he suggested I not let the other children be around him.*
>
> *Rachael and the children will set up a bed downstairs to the back corner of the hat shop and stay there for now. I survived the fever when I was two, but John Neal could not nurse my milk after he was born. He did not get my immunities passed to him like I did from my Mom. I am afraid.*

August 9, 1824

Young John Neal became lifeless and died as the mantel clock struck eleven. Frances was unable to comprehend how John Neal had been playing in mud puddles just a few days before and now was gone. Her mind raced to find a reason, and she realized that perhaps his illness was caused by the mosquitos from the ships that gathered around the moist mud and contaminated him with the fever. But she would never know. However, she would tell other families of the danger.

She sat almost lifeless by his bed, unable to stop her painful tears. Realizing she must react quickly to protect the other children, Frances opened the tall windows in the hearth room and called out to a neighbor to send the doctor. She went back to sit beside John Neal. In shock, she sat watching and hoping his lifeless chest would rise again to breath and wishing with all that was within her soul that he wasn't dead.

But she knew he was gone. She picked up his yellowed hand and held it to her heart. Even when her husband died, she had never felt as much pain.

The doctor came in to help her and advised her to keep the other children away for two weeks. He told her John's body must be buried as quickly as possible and to burn all the bed linens.

After young John Neal's body was taken away, Frances rolled the linens, but something fell from them and hit the floor—her brother, John Neal's, favorite writing pen and some folded paper. Young John Neal had been writing a letter to his Uncle John.

As Frances picked up the paper and pen, uncontrollable tears ran down her face. She wondered how tonight when she got on her knees beside her bed she could utter the words, "I thank you, heavenly Father, for another good day that has come and gone." Only God could give her the strength she needed.

January 19, 1825

My heart is still broken, and I cannot get over John Neal's death. I am hurting so deeply by his sudden death, and I feel I cannot go on. I need some sunshine from heaven on these dreary winter days as a reminder that God is still with me.

This afternoon America's French hero, General Lafayette, is in town. He is on a tour of honor for his service to the United State during and after the Revolutionary War. My papa served with him during many battles. To honor Papa, I will make myself get out. I must take the children to the parade. We will even go early to get a good place so the children can see him. I have told them many times the stories about General Lafayette that my Papa told me as we sat by the hearth fire. It is very cold today, but I will put peppermint and cookies in their pockets as a special treat. For now, I must get ready.

January 19, 1825

Each US city General Lafayette was scheduled to visit honored him in the most elaborate ways. The city of Baltimore built a special "Lafayette carriage" for his use only. The streets were lined with thousands of people hoping to get a glimpse of the general. Many American families have a story about the general coming to help America in their hour of need against the British. His willing heart and wisdom in battle made him a hero to all, second only to President George Washington.

Frances and her children sat on the curb early so they'd be sure to be able to see General Lafayette. They sat for a long time, and then suddenly, they heard a commotion up the street. The parade was about to begin.

Eight beautiful white horses elegantly stepped out to pull the carriage of America's hero. As he got close to where Frances and her children are standing, they stepped forward and saluted the General in honor of their grandfather, Frances's Papa. He looked toward them with a smile and raised his head. He gave a nod of approval and saluted them back.

Another memory was made.

CHAPTER 8

January 1, 1826

It is not yet sunrise on this snowy New Year's Day. Unable to sleep, I came to sit by the fading smoldering fire. I am cold, lonely, and sad. The thought of a new year only makes me sadder. I want my husband and John Neal back with us. I try with all my heart to be happy, but after John Neal died so suddenly, it seems impossible. His death has left a deep scar on George, Jane Ann, and Thomas's young hearts. I do not know if any of us can get past our heartache. God is our only comfort.

Not having a father, and my brother now in London, they need a man's influence in their life. They need a father. I must be determined to move forward. A widow for nearly eight years, I miss having a man to love and to love me. As difficult as it may be, I will ask God to bring a good, Godly man into my life for my children and for me.

I have sat in pity long enough. My children need me, and I need them. They will be awake soon, so I will throw a log on the fire to warm the house and bake the raised cinnamon rolls for their New Year's morning surprise. I choose to go forward one day at a time. With God at my side, I will not fail.

January 1, 1826

A New Year was not a comforting thought for Frances Catts. It had been more than a year since her son, John Neal Catts, passed away and almost eight years since her husband, John Catts, died. Sadness and sorrow ate away at her heart in silence. Would happiness ever fill her heart again? She had hit the bottom of the deep cistern in pain.

While her children slept, she cried alone in the dark almost every night. Pity took hold and seemed to be strangling Frances. She knew she must choose to break free from the chains of her sorrow.

Before sunrise on New Year's morning, after another sleepless night of grieving, Frances went into her children's room. Seeing their angelic faces lying against the white pillow covers on their down-filled beds, tears again filled her eyes.

She leaned over to kiss Thomas on his cheek. He opened his eyes and reached up to hug his mother. Holding him close, she realized she had three children who still needed her, and she needed them even more.

Her chains of sadness were broken. It was a New Year and a new beginning for Frances.

February 8, 1826

The day is done and gone is the sun. Today was my birthday, and it was filled with fun. Early this morning before I was fully awake, I heard someone moving around in my room. I was afraid, so I stayed quiet and laid very still. Barely opening one eye, I could see my children stirring around my room. I moved around in my bed and turned over. I could hear their giggles.

Suddenly, I sat up in bed and said, "Who is in my room?"

Three voices at once said, "Surprise! Happy birthday, Mama." They all piled on my bed, giving me a giant hug. My heart melted.

On my side table was a rose china plate piled high with muffins. Next to it was my Mama's china tea cup with my favorite hot tea. Across the foot of my bed I saw three gifts.

Seeing that Thomas was most excited, I asked if I could open his gift first. I complimented the wrapping paper which he had colored with pink flowers and tied with a pink ribbon. When I asked if he would help me open his gift, he smiled from ear to ear. Pulling it open, I saw a wooden sign. He read the words to me, "Frances Catts, Owner, Catts Fine Millinery Shop." I am not sure who was more pleased, Thomas or me.

Jane Ann handed me her gift in a hat box from the shop. On the side was written, "Jane Ann's Fine Hats." She had tied it with a big white ribbon, also from the shop. Pulling on the ribbon and lifting the lid, I found the most beautiful hat I had ever seen. It had rows of pink pleats above a wide brim, a slightly darker pink braid, and delicate white lace roses on one side. And on the side, she had stuck a hat pin she made with glass buttons and beads. She told me she had been working on the hat at night with scraps from the shop.

Leaning over, I gave her a big hug and told her how proud I was of her work. She placed it on my head which I'm sure looked nice with my nightgown.

George waited with his gift at the end of the bed. It was small, wrapped in white paper, and tied with a lavender ribbon. Handing it to me, he gave a boyish smile. Pulling away the ribbon and paper, I found a bottle of perfume. I opened the top and the smell of lavender filled the room.

George said, "I remember Papa calling you his Lavender Lady. I've been shoveling snow for Mr. Turner at the mercantile store. When I saw the lavender perfume, he let me buy for you it at a good price." He leaned down to give me a hug. I hugged him so tightly.

I spent the entire day with my children, hugging them more than I had hugged them in a long time. As I sit in my bed writing about the day, my birthday, I thank God for my children. I will write my prayer to God tonight, one that I have not been able to pray in some time.

I thank You, heavenly Father, for another good day that has come and gone.

July 4, 1826

Today we celebrated fifty years of independence from the British. My Papa fought for our freedom and so did my husband John. This will be the biggest celebration ever. My hat shop is closed, and I will spend the day with my children, teaching them that America is a blessed nation by God. I got the piece of the Star-Spangled Banner flag out of the box and let each of them hold the loosely woven wool fabric while I told the story of the flag. Proudly, I told them about their Papa serving in the war.

Together, we packed a basket to take for supper on the ground at Fort McHenry. We will stay late to see the biggest fireworks show ever in America. We will hear lots of music, including our beloved song, "The Star-Spangled Banner." When I hear it being sung, I think of Frankie and the day he read his poem to me as we walked in the garden. Sweet memories never grow old.

July 4, 1826

All across America, people celebrated fifty years of freedom and independence.

Sadly, former presidents Thomas Jefferson and John Adams died within hours of one another on this day, exactly fifty years after they signed the Declaration of Independence.

> *November 23, 1826*
> *I am up early cooking two turkeys. One is for our family, and one for a long-time friend who brought his wife to see a doctor in Baltimore. She has been sick for over a year. I pray that Doctor Garrett will be able to help her. They have been staying with friends the last two weeks. I sent word to them that we will deliver their Thanksgiving meal by eleven o'clock. Jane Ann is going to make an apple pie, George will roast sweet potatoes. And Thomas will cook green beans. Rachael has already made a cake. We will make double of everything so our meal is ready to have when we return.*
> *We are thankful to have enough to share.*

November 23, 1826

The Catts family always helped others. A long-time family friend from Wellsburg, Virginia, Thomas Crawford brought his wife, Helen, to see a specialist doctor. Her health had been frail for months, and her doctor has been unable to help her. Thomas was a friend of John Catts during the War of 1812.

> *April 25, 1827*
> *I received a letter from Thomas Crawford, letting me know his wife, Helen, passed away on April 11. He is devastated and asked that we pray for his four sons and for him. He cannot imagine life without her or that he will be able to raise his sons alone.*
> *I know what he is feeling, and my prayers will be with them.*

April 25, 1827

Thomas Crawford, Esq. was a successful lawyer and gentlemen farmer from Virginia. His farm along the Buffalo

Creek adjoined the land of Alexander Campbell, the founder of the Christian Church and later Bethany College. Campbell, also an educator, taught boys' Latin, Greek, and writing in his home before he established the college. Thomas's boys would climb the white-railed fence separating the farms and go to Campbell's home to study.

Thomas had apple orchards on his farm, and he started apple trees for other people to grow.

His wife, Helen, was from the Hammond family. She was the third daughter of fifteen children. Education was a priority to families that could afford to have tutors for their children. The Hammond family homeschooled and later had all their children tutored. Helen's brother was a lawyer in Ohio was asked to serve as a Supreme Court Judge. Not having sons of his own, he hoped one of his sisters' sons would study law one day with him.

May 23, 1827

My son, John Neal Catts, would have been twelve years old today. I will never stop missing him. Instead of being sad, we will celebrate. Together, we will bake a birthday cake and remember good stories about his life. He is buried beside his Papa, so we will put flowers on both of their graves and sing songs of joy over them.

I will teach the children to be thankful in all things. God gave me a good husband and precious children. And he gave us John Neal. If only for a short time, he was ours to love. I choose to be thankful for the time God allowed us to be a family. And we will continue to be a family.

May 23, 1827

Frances's heart had changed. Not that she wanted it to happen, but she accepted her life. She wrote a sympathy letter to Thomas Crawford. Perhaps, because she knew what he was feeling, he was on Frances's heart and in her prayers. She remembered her husband, John, had great respect for Thomas Crawford.

Frances knew God chooses who will live and who will die. Sometimes, all was not well in her heart because she no longer had John Neal or John, but in her soul she was well. She was finally at peace. Tonight, she could again say she was thankful for another good day.

September 10, 1827

It has rained for the last three days. I sent George to the Mercantile to pick up four pair of rubber galoshes. I read about them in the newspaper. They are rubber boots that will keep your feet dry in the rain. If it has stopped raining when he returns, we are going to try our new boots to see if they really work. We will splash and jump in the rain puddles on our street. I am not sure who will have the most fun, Thomas or me. We will make another memory.

September 10, 1827

The gloominess of three days of rain made Frances feel the sadness of life creep back into her heart. She could feel her grief start to take hold. Determined not to go down that road again, she ordered rubber galoshes. She would rather catch a cold in the rain than go back to the darkness of self-pity. She had learned the hard way to be on guard.

God had changed her heartache into a thankful heart.

December 1, 1828

I have never seen Thomas so happy. Our family friends, the Crawfords, came to Baltimore three days ago with their father for business. We celebrated Thomas Love's birthday early. I invited the Crawfords for lunch and birthday cake. Since it was cold and snowy, I offered for us to sit in the hearth room by the fire. However, the Crawford boys had a different idea. They bundled up and grabbed a broken broom handle. They drew broom straws to divide into teams and headed to the side yard for a game of stick ball.

Thomas Crawford and I stood by the kitchen window watching them pack snow balls for the game. We could hear them laughing and having fun. The birthday boy got to hit first. They shattered snowball after snowball with the broomstick. Jane Ann, the only girl, fit right in with the six boys.

Turning to me, Thomas asked for his coat. Smiling, he also asked me to get mine. We went out the front door and made snow balls. We stacked them by the corner of the house. Then we snuck around the side and pelted the boys and Jane Ann with snowballs. It was a battle to the end. And they won.

Once back inside by the fire, we finished Thomas's birthday cake with warm coco milk.

I am excited to get on my knees tonight. With joy in my heart, I began, "I thank you, heavenly Father, for another good day that has come and gone." I am thankful my brother, John Neal, is home from London. And grateful to God that better days are ahead.

December 1, 1828

Searching for excuses to go to Baltimore on business or to visit his brother, Thomas Crawford enjoyed more time with Frances Catts. The two families were meshing together well. George Catts and Robert Crawford were born eighteen days apart, so they quickly became like brothers. Jane Ann could hold her own with all the boys. And Thomas L. soaked in the extra attention Thomas Crawford gave him. Two families were becoming one.

July 4, 1828

I woke up thinking about the day I married John Catts. We would have been married eighteen years today. I am thirty-six years old, and he would have been forty-one in just a few days. He has been gone for ten years. I think he would be proud of our children. George has a business mind and is wise. Jane Ann has a servant's heart to help everyone and far exceeds my ability in sewing. Thomas will soon be eleven and has a heart for adventure. I can only imagine the plan God has for them. I will start my day with a thankful heart.

Jane Ann has planned our Independence Day picnic. We will include Thomas Crawford and his sons for our picnic and the fireworks tonight. He is in town for the ground breaking of the first commercial railroad, the Baltimore and Ohio. His law office secured the land, and he was asked to attend a breakfast and the *ceremony. Thomas invited me to go with him. I made a new blue dress and hat to wear with a matching purse. To my surprise, I am excited to see him.*

July 4, 1828

Thomas Crawford frequently came to Baltimore on business. He was coming more often now that over a year had gone by since his wife, Helen, passed away. He brought with him alterations to drop off at the "Catts Fine Millinery Shop." Plenty of ladies in Wellsburg could've done his alterations, but he wanted an excuse to visit Frances.

The ground breaking of the Baltimore and Ohio Rail Road would have tremendous impact on the city. More growth and more people were certain to happen. Baltimore, one of the largest cities in America, and perhaps the largest port city, was getting too big for Frances.

The Catts and Crawford children secured immediate friendships. Having met several times in past years, they were comfortable spending time together. Thomas and Frances were pleased to see their families get along so well. They too were also getting along quite well.

May 5, 1829

I have many decisions to make. Our family has been invited to the Crawford farm in Virginia. My long-distance friendship with Thomas is about to change. I pray God will guide my heart to make wise decisions.

May 5, 1829

Thomas Crawford invited the Catts family to visit their farm in Virginia. He also asked his extended family to come, so they could meet Frances. His sister would come early to prepare for perhaps her brother's new bride.

CHAPTER 9

May 12, 1829

I cannot sleep, so I will write my thoughts about Thomas. Being at his farm and meeting his family is a good feeling for me. I am tired of living in the city, and I do want a quieter life. I am not sure adding the responsibility of four boys and a husband will quiet my life, but I know I have fallen in love with Thomas. The many responsibilities of the hat shop seem to be a burden to me now. I am forever grateful it provided for my family after John died and grateful my mother taught me to sew and to make hats.

Rachael, still unmarried, would like to buy the shop and our house. She has saved her money since she has had only herself to consider. My brother, John Neal, has assured me he will be there to help her if needed. I will be sad to leave John and Rachael, but I did ask God to bring someone into my life who would love my children as John did.

I think Thomas is the man God has chosen. He has a good heart and is a godly man I can trust. He has asked that George, Jane Ann, and Thomas call him Papa. This has made young Thomas very happy since he was only a few months old when his father died. I will be very sad to leave behind the graves of my first husband, John, and our son John Neal. I will wait for God to guide my decisions.

May 12, 1829

The apple trees are a little late blooming in Wellsburg. For Frances Catts and Thomas Crawford, his apple orchard was a beautiful place to walk as they discussed their future. Knowing that combining two families would be challenging, Thomas suggested they sit under an apple tree to pray. This was the first time since before John died that Frances felt loved.

June 19, 1829

Our wedding is planned for tomorrow, June 15. I am happy, and our children are happy—all of them. I will go from being a mother of three to a mother of seven in just a few hours. Thomas has been patient in helping me leave my home in Baltimore. He knows I have special treasures from my past that I cannot leave behind, especially the sign John carved for me for Christmas. Thomas would like for it to go on our mantel as a commitment to our future, "In God is our trust." God has been with me in my darkest days, and he will be with us as we step out in faith for our future.

I cried when I said goodbye to Rachael and John. She had a new sign made for the shop. Wrapped in white paper as a gift was the sign, "Catts Fine Millinery Shop," ready to take with me. I had already packed the sign Thomas made for my birthday. I gave John and Rachael many of our family heirlooms. My brother, John, reminded me that he would like George to have his silver pocket watch when he turns twenty-one.

The children and I will enjoy living on the Crawford farm. We have already met Pastor Alexander Campbell. Starting in the fall, George and Thomas will attend school at the Campbell house with Thomas's boys. Jane Ann will attend a girl's finishing school. Life will be different here, and I will work hard to be a good wife for Thomas.

I must get some sleep. My prayers will be many tonight.

June 19, 1829

Frances Catts sold her house and her hat shop to her sister. She packed her belongings on a wagon for her move to Virginia. Although difficult, she said goodbye to her brother and sister. She was confident in her love for Thomas Crawford and in his love for her children. And thankful God answered her prayer

June 20, 1829

I thank you heavenly Father for this day, our wedding day, a new beginning for Thomas and me.

June 20, 1829

A cool breeze gently swayed the leaves on the big red maple trees as the afternoon sun sparkled rays of hope from heaven onto an arbor covered in climbing blue hydrangea flowers. Thomas Crawford and Frances Catts stepped forward with their seven children arched around them to promise they would love each other until the day they die.

The few family and guests applauded with approval. Six young boys and one teenage girl jumped and hollered with excitement.

After cake and punch, Thomas and Frances rode away in a carriage with six tin cans tied on the back and one pink bow.

Later that evening, Robert and George went down by the creek to skip rocks. They were happy their parents were married and they were now brothers. Robert pulled a knife from his pocket, cut his thumb and handed the knife to George, who also cut his thumb. By pressing their thumbs together and rubbing their blood together, they promised to be blood brothers forever.

Frances definitely thanked God that night for another good day.

September 12, 1829

The house is quiet, six boys and Jane Ann are at school. I have work to do, but I will sit to have a cup of tea for just a few moments. My happy days are here again. I am thankful to be Mrs. Thomas Crawford and for our family to be together. We have had some bumps in the road adjusting to one another's personalities, but everyone is working together. Thomas is good to ask questions during our meals so we learn more about one another. He has the boys picking apples in the afternoons after school. Finding the rotten apples to throw at each other makes their work fun.

Thomas L, as we now call him, is keeping up with his older brothers, and I am glad they include him. I watch as they climb the white fence each morning and run across the green field to school. I am pleased they have the opportunity to study writing and Latin.

Jane Ann has made friends at the girl's finishing school and shares all she is learning about manners.

I have finished my tea, and bushels of apples are waiting to sort. Saturday Thomas has promised to teach me how to make apple butter in a copper kettle.

Thomas knows the more time the family spends working together, the more they will depend on each other. Life on the Crawford farm will prepare Frances for what is in her future.

December 24, 1829

Our family gathered in the hearth room after the candlelight service at church to sing. The voices of the boys are changing. They laughed at one another as their voices would go high and low. Sweet Jane Ann tried to stay quiet but finally burst out in laughter at her six brothers singing. I noticed Thomas looking at their faces, and he would smile. I think he is surprised at how quickly we have become one family. By Robert's suggestion a month ago, we drew names from a hat to make a gift for one another. He drew Jane Ann's name and has been secretly working at night on her gift. I am anxious to see what he has made for her. I made Thomas a new black hat and coat. I hope he is pleased.

A bushel of apples from the cellar is sitting by the hearth as a winter treat. Thomas has the tradition of telling the story of the star over Bethlehem with an apple. New to his family, we will hear it for the first time. With his pocket knife, he cut across the side of the apple and showed them how the placement of the seeds forms a star in the center. He explained God made the apples with the star to remind us of the star over Bethlehem that shinned so brightly the night Jesus was born.

Thomas looked at Thomas L. and said, "You can always use an apple to tell the story about Jesus." Then he added, "That is why I have apple orchards. Only God knows how many apples are in each seed and how many times his story will be told."

Thomas got everyone's attention so he could read from the Bible. Reading from the second chapter of Luke, he began, "And it came to pass in those days ..." In the quiet stillness of the moment, as we sat by the warm fire as a family, my heart called out in praise, "I thank you, heavenly Father, for another good day."

December 24, 1829

This was the first Christmas Eve as one family—the Catts/Crawford family. The sign carved by John Catts with the words of Francis Scott Key's poem "In God is our trust" had been placed on the mantel the day Thomas and Frances got married. The words now were illuminated by the candles on each side of the mantel and the warm light from the fire. Two families committed to those words shared their first Christmas together.

June 20, 1830

So excited, I am unable to sleep. I came to sit by the fire so as not to keep Thomas awake. Today is our one-year anniversary. At supper tonight, I shocked everyone. I announced that we are going to have a baby. There was silence. Not a word from the boys or Jane Ann. Finally, Thomas leaned over, kissed my cheek and patted my hand. Smiles covered all faces. Thomas L. is so happy he will be a big brother, especially since he was a little brother to five older brothers. Thomas is happy we will have "our" child

June 20, 1830

The boys have finished one year of school, and Jane Ann has no classes for summer. Thinking it would be a quiet summer, the announcement of a new baby caused quite a commotion in the Catts/Crawford family.

February 14, 1831

I had the Valentine cookies wrapped for Thomas to put under the children's pillows. Even if they are older, they still look for cookies under their pillow. Robert and George are home for two weeks from their academy classes and Thomas L. is glad to have time with his brothers. Jane Ann thinks it is best to be home with me. Thomas's sister came to stay until after the baby is born. Everyone is keeping an eye on me.

We loaded into two buggies to go for church on this cold Sunday morning. Pastor was in the middle of preaching when I felt a pain in my lower back. I moved to get comfortable, but the pain hit again. Grabbing Thomas's hand and squeezing hard, I easily conveyed to him that my time had come. We stood up, as did the rest of our family. With everyone watching, we quickly marched out of church like a parade.

The short ride home was difficult. As soon as we got inside the house, I got into bed. Thomas, Jane Ann, and Thomas's sister came in with me. As my pains increased and time for delivery drew *closer, Thomas went out into the hearth room to sit. He and our boys took turns pacing back and forth. Time was slow in passing, but finally our baby began to cry.*

Thomas came into the room, and the boys followed, hovering around the end of the bed. Charles Hammond Crawford was first held by his father and then by Jane Ann. Each of the boys waited for their turn to hold their new brother

Thomas L. was first to speak out saying, "I think I'll call him Charlie."

February 14, 1831

Frances was thirty-nine and Thomas was forty-nine years old when Charles was born.

October 28, 1831

Thomas asked me today if I would like to move out west. With little Charles in my arms, I did not know what to say. Confused, I only looked at my husband.

October 28, 1831

The United States Government announced they would begin to open land for homesteading west of the Mississippi River. Thomas caught the bug like so many others to go west.

Robert left in August to attend West Point Military Academy in New York. He wouldn't be allowed to come home for two years. He wrote often to George and to Jane Ann.

George and the other boys continued their studies with Alexander Campbell and at the academy.

Jane Ann finished at the girls' academy in the spring.

Heading west became a topic of conversation every evening at the supper table.

February 14, 1832

Charles is one-year old today. Only Thomas L. is home for his little brother's birthday. He has carved him a wooden horse, a cow, and a goat so they can play together on the floor. Jane Ann made a sock doll for Charles, and I sewed him a new coat. Thomas hopes to finish in court early so he can come home. He and Thomas L. have built a rocking horse for Charles. I am sad everyone else is away at school and will miss his birthday. We will still celebrate, and Thomas L. is glad there will be more cake for him.

February 14, 1832

Thomas and Frances saw their boys growing up and starting a new life. George worked part time and attended school. Uncle Charles Hammond officially recommended Robert to West Point Military Academy. Charles was the brother of Robert's mother, a judge in Ohio. He had been asked by the president to serve as a Supreme Court judge but declined. Robert was considering a military career and was delighted to have the opportunity to attend West Point. He was unhappy, however, that he will be given no leave for the first two years.

Thomas hoped Robert would read law and perhaps partner in his or his uncle's law practice. The other boys were busy making plans for their future.

Only Thomas L. and Charles were home with Thomas and Frances.

The family sent cards and for Charles's first birthday. Frances and Thomas were somewhat saddened to see empty chairs for his party.

Thomas talked more about going west.

August 15, 1833

We are planning a big celebration for Robert when he comes home from West Point next week. Even his uncle Charles Hammond will come from Cincinnati to welcome him home. George missed his brother and will be glad to have him home. Jane Ann is excited to see Robert. I think he will be surprised to see her all grown up. Thomas L. has made Robert a wooden box with his name carved on top to keep his pens and pencils in. Little Charles, now two and a half years old, sadly does not know Robert. The other brothers plan to be home.

Thomas is most excited to see Robert and wants to hear about his future plans. I am certain the topic will come up about going west. As for me, I am beginning to understand why Thomas wants to go. Our farm here in Virginia can be run by our other sons since they are certain they want to stay in Virginia. George has a good business mind and hopes to one day own a mercantile in town. Thomas has taught Thomas L. all there is to know about the apple orchards. And he knows the story about the star in the center of the apple.

I know life is changing for our family. I choose to be thankful for each time we are together.

August 15, 1833

Robert has been at West Point for two years. The other boys are close enough to come home frequently. Knowing in advance he must agree to stay for the first two years without leave, Robert committed himself to the program because that's what he wanted. He'd be a man when he returned. Thomas would be happy to have his son home even if only for a short time.

August 25, 1832

Before going back to Ohio, Uncle Charles Hammond invited Robert to come to Cincinnati to read law with him. Thomas is pleased and thinks it is a good decision. George is glad Robert will be closer to home. While sitting out on the porch, he and Robert told us the story about when they cut their thumbs and rubbed their blood together so they would be forever blood brothers. They are good encouragement to each other. I hope they will always stay close as brothers.

I told Thomas I will agree to go west. If that is his dream, I will go with him.

August 25, 1832

Robert made his move to Cincinnati to live with his uncle. All the boys came home to help Thomas and Frances with their decision and plan to move west. Some of them would go west to Missouri to scout out the best area to homestead and to find out when the land would be made available.

CHAPTER 10

September 30, 1833

Thomas is happy all of the boys are home to help with apple picking. It is good to see them working together again. Robert and George are now twenty-one, but they are still like the young boys they were when we first came to the farm. They look for rotten apples to throw at one another. Jane Ann is home to help keep an eye on Charles and to help make apple butter in the big copper kettles. If she is home long enough, we will can apples for pies and make applesauce for winter.

Not having seen each other very often in the last few years, Robert and Jane Ann are spending more time together. He later told George that he thinks Jane Ann is beautiful.

We had a family meeting tonight to discuss going west. Thomas will leave the farm in Virginia for the boys who want to stay behind. He wants to make sure they will always have a home. Jane Ann can choose if she wants to go. Thomas L, now sixteen, and little Charles will go with Thomas and me in a covered wagon to Missouri. We will leave next spring and stop in Cincinnati to visit family.

I have mixed feelings about our decision, but I have assured Thomas where he goes, I will go.

September 30, 1833

The decision for families to go west wasn't made lightly. The women were more fearful for their family, but the men saw it as an adventure they would regret if they didn't go. Had they not gone, America would never have expanded. Each wagon that rolled west made a trail for someone to come behind them to also follow their dream.

December 24, 1833

This will be our last candlelight church service with friends and our last Christmas as a family on our farm in Virginia. We have gone through family keepsakes and have written names on who will receive each item. And instead of making gifts, we are giving family treasures for Christmas.

George could not come home for his twenty-first birthday, so I have wrapped my brother, John Neal's, silver pocket watch for him. Thomas L. will get my Papa's *silver compass. Jane Ann will be given my Mama's trunk. Thomas will give Robert the watch* *that belonged to his mother's father. Young Charles will one day have the watch that belonged to Thomas's father. The other boys will have the farm and the furniture. They have agreed to share the profits with all of the family until we are established in the west.*

Tonight is the last night here in Virginia for Thomas to tell the story of the Bethlehem star and to read about the birth of Jesus from our family Bible. As I look at each face, I am sad that this is our last Christmas together. I then look up at the sign on the mantel, "In God is our trust." I find myself repeating those words over and over again as the day gets closer to our leaving.

Thomas L. has learned to play the fiddle quiet well. He ended our Christmas Eve evening with music. Little Charles grabbed his Papa's hand to dance with him around the Christmas tree.

December 24, 1833

Preparing to go west became one of the most difficult tasks for any family, and the Crawford's were no different. Once they left, there was usually no going back. To sort their family heirlooms and treasures and to face the reality they may never see one another again was heartbreaking.

June 1, 1834

We are later in leaving than planned, but along the way there is a wedding we want to attend. Robert has been in Cincinnati for the last year studying law with his uncle. He has come home every opportunity he can to see Jane Ann. They have fallen in love and will be married in September. Some of the ladies at church gossip about them being stepbrother and sister, yet they know there is no blood relation between them. Thomas said to let them gossip, but we will choose to be happy for them. Robert has been away for most of the last three years.

Jane Ann and I have made a beautiful wedding dress, and she has it in my Mama's trunk with other special family items. She will go with us tomorrow to Cincinnati and stay with us at a relative's house until the wedding. Afterward, she will go with Robert, and we will continue going west to Missouri.

George has decided to stay. I am not sure I will be able to say goodbye to him. He has promised if Missouri is as wonderful as Papa hopes it will be, he will move there also. But he will first find his bride to take with him. As expected, the other boys are staying too. Thomas and I both will have difficulty in saying goodbye to all who stay behind as well as neighbors and so many friends.

Thomas and Thomas L. took a walk through the apple orchards early this morning. Thomas has labored to plant the orchards and has worked the land for many years. His sweat is in the dirt, and his heart is in seeing the apple trees grow to produce fruit. After their walk, Thomas pulled a small box with a sliding lid from his pocket. He showed Thomas L. the star of an apple carved on the lid. The box was full of apple seeds. His father had carved the box for him when he bought the farm. Placing it in Thomas L.'s hand to keep, he reminded him that only God knows how many apples are in each seed.

I watched Thomas walk from room to room in our house with sadness in his eyes. He built the house with his father's help. It has taken him all week to say goodbye to the people he has helped through his law office. I know the heartache he feels. I left my home where I was born to come to Virginia. I feel in my heart that most likely I will never see my sister and brother again or my friend Francis Scott Key. We are all filled with sadness tonight.

Our wagon is packed with only the things we will need for travel. Food and water must find a place in the wagon, then, if there is room, we will take what we can. Thomas L. made a wooden box with a cross carved on top so our family Bible will travel safely. I missed seeing where the sign "In God is our trust" was packed until tonight. Realizing my concern, Thomas took me out to the wagon to show me where he put the sign for safe keeping. He attached it to the footboard where we will rest our feet on the front of our wagon. He said our feet will rest on the words, "In God is our trust," as we travel. We will trust God to take us where  he wants us to go and to take care of our family we leave behind.

At sunrise we will hitch up our team of mules, tie a milk cow and a horse to the back of the wagon, and wave goodbye to our family until they are out of sight. We will then look forward to our new home.

September 15, 1834

It was a lovely wedding for Robert and Jane Ann yesterday. She looked beautiful in her wedding dress, and Robert is a handsome man. As with telling George goodbye, it is almost unbearable to tell Jane Ann and Robert goodbye. Thomas said he thinks a woman's tears are even deeper than the deepest water well.

Thomas L. has kept little Charles entertained today. With each stop, he finds a piece of wood to carve for him. He has walked most of the day, gathering wood to pitch on the possum-belly of our wagon so we will have wood for a fire when we stop for the night. Uncertain how far we can travel each day, we hope to cross the Mississippi River before the cold weather sets in. If not, we will wait until early spring to cross before the rainy season.

Our milk cow must be tired from the long walk. She gave very little milk for Charles to drink with supper. We will use our food sparingly and hope to find fresh meat along the trail. I packed fresh eggs in a barrel of corn meal so we will have eggs and salt pork on Sunday morning.

I was comforted when I saw our sign on the front step of our wagon this morning. We may need the reminder of those words many times before we reach Missouri.

The fire has burned down for the night and I am tired. I will turn down the oil lantern so I can go to sleep. With all of us sleeping inside, the wagon is so full I cannot get on my knees to pray. I will fall asleep praying, "I thank you, heavenly Father, for another good day that has come and gone."

September 15, 1834

Travel by covered wagon was hard and painful. The trail was often so rough. Riding in the wagon became harder than walking. The Crawfords would take months to travel the one-thousand miles to Missouri.

October 24, 1834

We made it to Saint Genevieve, Missouri, where we crossed the Mississippi river on a ferry. We had to unload the wagon, take the wheels off, and load it onto the ferry. Our livestock, the mules, the horse, and the cow had to ride separately. Holding little Charles tightly in my arms, I kept repeating the words that were close by me on the step. Thomas L. thought it was an exciting ride. We safely made it to the other side.

While standing on the side waiting for our wagon to be unloaded from the ferry, another family was on a ferry behind us. The entire family traveled with their livestock instead of going with their wagon. A large log in the swift water slammed into the ferry causing one of their mules to rear up. Scaring the other animals, they moved to one side.

In horror, we watched as the ferry toppled over. Thomas and other men jumped into the water to try to pull the people from the rushing water. They saved only two of the children. The parents and two other children drowned. I covered Thomas L. and Charles's eyes so they would not see the bodies pulled from the water.

Since all of their belonging were lost in the river, there was probably no way to locate family members. I asked if I could care for the children until someone could find them a home. The ferry workers agreed. Unloading our wagon and livestock took a long time, and the wheels had to be packed in mule grease and put back on the wagon.

Everyone's heart hurt as the two boys cried for their Mama.

I have already told Thomas I will refuse to leave Saint Genevieve until I find a home for the two homeless boys. They will sleep in the wagon with us tonight and Thomas L. has agreed to sleep on the possum-belly under the wagon. The boys continue to cry so I will cry with them until we fall asleep.

October 24, 1834

The unexpected disasters along the trail brought fear to those around them. To go west meant the powerful Mississippi River had to be crossed. Thomas took his family south to cross at the shallowest part of the river near Saint Genevieve. But the mighty river had a mind of its own. If there were heavy rains north of Saint Louis, the river would swell out of the banks farther south in just a few hours. Any accidents in the water were usually disastrous. All families that reached safety across the river thanked God his protection.

Saint Genevieve, a French Trading Post, was a good place for the Catts/Crawford family to spend the winter. Careful not to put his family in danger during winter through unknown areas to travel, Thomas made the decision to stay. They found a pioneer camp outside of town where they had the support and help of other families if needed. Thomas L. learned to hunt and fish with Thomas Crawford that winter. As soon as the warm days of spring came, they were ready to continue west.

February 8, 1835

We are still in Saint Genevieve, camped outside of town with other families. It took a long time to find someone to care for Willie and Pete. One of the ladies at the church told me a quiet single lady who ran a boarding house lived alone and that maybe she would take the children. At first when I went to see her, she was angry that I had bothered her. She had never told anyone her husband and three children had been killed when their house burned near Cape Girardeau ten years before. She had silently grieved with no one to talk to and no family.

Later, she saw me in town with the boys, and I noticed she was crying. I asked Thomas L. to take Willie and Pete to get a candy stick while I talked with Mrs. Sammon. Charles was at the wagon with Thomas.

As soon as we sat down, she broke down. She told me the story about her family. She had gone up in the woods to pick blackberries to make a pie for their supper. She smelled smoke, ran out of the woods, and could see the smoke rising from her house. She ran through the tall grass field but by the time she got there, it was too late. All these years, she was haunted by the question as to why they could not get out of the house. Leaning over, she covered her face with her hands

Feeling her sadness, I thought more than likely, her hands had overflowed many times with her tears. Not realizing Mrs. Sammon was still crying, Thomas L. walked up with the boys.

When Willie saw her crying, he ran to her and gave her a hug.

Little Pete went to stand beside her. Holding her hand and patting her back, he said, "We're going to be ok."

She grabbed both the boys, and they were hers from that moment on.

We have weathered through a cold winter here and found a good home for Willie and Pete. So, we will move west when warm weather comes. I promised Mrs. Sammon I would write to her when we are settled. I never once thought about today being my birthday. But I think God gave me a good gift. I will fall asleep tonight praying for Pete and Willie and their new Mama.

February 8, 1835

Many children were left homeless along the westward trails. Willie and Pete were saved from the rushing waters of the river for a purpose. They gave comfort to a lady they did not know. She became the new Mama they cried for. The west was a wild, unforgiving place, and the people had to be strong to keep moving west. Neighbors were more than neighbors. They were part of a larger family who looked out for one another.

May 1, 1835

The warm sunshine feels good as we travel in our wagon. Little Charles, now four-years old, is learning bird calls from Thomas L. It keeps them busy during the long day. Three families we met at the trading post are not far behind. For safety, we will camp together each night. Thomas has made friends with an Indian. He watches us from a distance as if he wants to be sure we are safe. We will go north tomorrow until we find a lower stream of the Meramec River. Here Thomas thinks we should camp for a while.

I will be able to wash clothes, clean the wagon, and take a much-needed bath in the stream.

The mules and the horse are spent earlier each day. Thomas thinks a week of grazing and fresh water will make them strong again. Mosey, as Charles has named our cow, needs to graze on the fine Missouri grass also. Thomas L. has seen turkeys in the fields. He hopes to get one for tomorrow's supper.

By evening I am very tired. Either I cook at noon to have enough food for supper, or if the men bring meat, then I cook enough for several days. For a city gal, I have learned a lot.

I saw the most beautiful sight to behold yesterday. We stopped early beside a creek so we could fill our water barrels. I saw poke-greens at the edge of the woods and thought they would be a good for supper. I found plenty and was enjoying my carefree, much-needed walk. Deeper in the woods, I stopped. All around me, knee high, were white flowers. The plant they bloomed from had big leaves and pointed down. I'm not sure what they are but they were as beautiful as what I imagine a walk in heaven might be.

May 1, 1835

Pioneers from the East saw and experienced many unusual situations on the trails they had never traveled before. They learned to stay close to other families and to prepare always for the unexpected.

July 2, 1835

Thomas L. has been responsible to keep up with our days of travel. He assures me we have two days until Independence Day. Wherever we are, Thomas has promised we will stop for the day. He said to have our picnic ready. It will be good to rest and let Charles play. I feel certain we will not have beautiful fireworks. I often think of Rachael and John Neal. I hope they will enjoy the fireworks at the fort for me. So many memories I left behind.

July 2, 1835

Days quickly turned into weeks as exhaustion took over the people and the animals. Thomas was wise to be considerate of his family and allow them to rest. He stopped every Sunday so he could teach Thomas L. and Charles from the Bible. He added a history lesson on Sunday, teaching that our nation was founded with God's principals.

July 4, 1835

We found a beautiful spring to camp by for our picnic. Two families, the Campbells and the Fulbrights, have been camped here for some time. They hope to homestead this area. I cooked plenty of food, so we have invited them to celebrate Independence Day with us. Thomas L. is anxious to play his fiddle, and little Charles I'm sure will dance and sing. We are thankful to be at this place, and Thomas thinks we might stay a while. Some people build a one-room cabin, and when they move on, others can stay in the cabin.

CHAPTER 11

May 16, 1836

Springfield was home for the winter of 1835. We were thankful to move into a cabin the week before Christmas, just before another big snow. Thomas L. cut a small Scotch pine tree for our tiny cabin. Six-year-old Charles wanted a three-legged stool to sit on to milk Mosey, our cow. John Campbell saved fall apples in his cellar for Thomas L. to use to tell the story about the star over Bethlehem to all the children in town. On Christmas Eve, we sat by our warm fire listening as he read the Christmas story from our family Bible. Never saying a word, we all knew how much we missed others in our family.

Winter is behind us and the spring sunshine makes us feel good. Thomas and John Campbell have already scouted the next county for a place to homestead. Seeing the creeks were still high and some overflowing from melted snow and rain, we waited until May sixteenth to go west. We loaded our wagon, hitched up the mules, and again placed our feet on the buckboard step.

"In God is our trust!" Thomas yelled as we pulled out of Springfield.

I was surprised by the beautiful yellow forsythia edging the woods along the rolling hills. The white dogwood blooms and dark pink redbud trees, blooming later than normal, made me want to stop for a walk in the woods. But instead, we traveled on west. All but Thomas had to get off the wagon before the mules could pull it up a big hill. I closed my eyes as he held the reins tight and headed down the other side. Late in the day, we came to the creek John Campbell advised would be most difficult to cross. It was where others had turned back to Springfield.

Thomas slowly moved the mules to the swollen creek's edge. The rushing waters scared the mules and they began to back up. He yelled, "We've gotta turn back!" And we did. We too now call it, the Turn Back Creek.

Thomas said we will camp tonight along the wood's edge a good distance from the creek. He said he hoped I would fall in love with the beautiful rolling Ozark hills. And I did.

May 16, 1836

More settlers rolled their wagon west to Missouri for a place to homestead good rich farm land.

July 4, 1836

Today, America celebrated sixty years since the Declaration of Independence was signed. We are getting ready for our picnic by the spring. Thomas L. has carved three small boats to race in the creek. Charles has been practicing for the sack race and the one-legged race. I have cooked for the last three days. I am sure we will have a lovely day. But I miss home and I miss our family that is not with us. We receive a letter every now and again, saying they are all doing well. But I still miss them. I have written to Jane Ann and Robert, telling them how much we like Missouri and our neighbors who have helped us so much. Oh, how I wish they would come west to Missouri.

July 4, 1836

Jane Ann and Robert were already considering a move to Missouri. Robert will finish reading law with his Uncle Charles Hammond. When he asked Charles if he would be upset if he graciously refused his offer to practice law in Ohio, he replied, "If I can refuse to serve on the Supreme Court of the United States when asked by President John Quincy Adams, you, my dear nephew, can refuse my offer."

May 12, 1837

I received a letter from Jane Ann saying they will arrive around the middle of June. Thomas has built a cabin. We have an extra room for Robert and Jane Ann. Thomas L. is counting the days until they arrive. I sent him to the Mercantile for cornmeal and sugar. He returned in a wagon. Cautiously climbing down from the wagon was a young mother with a baby in her arms. When she turned around, I could see she was my Jane Ann. I rushed to her and she placed her baby in my arms.

She said, "Meet your new granddaughter, Helen Frances Crawford."

Thomas L. ran to get his Papa to come home. Charles jumped to hug his brother, Robert, and Jane Ann. When Thomas saw the baby, a tear rolled down his cheek. Jane Ann laid the baby in his arms and told him her name is Helen Frances. Helen was Robert's mother's name.

We celebrated for a week.

May 12, 1837

It's hard to imagine not seeing one's family for three years. Both Jane Ann and Robert were anxious to see their parents. They left Cincinnati earlier than planned. Jane Ann went into labor early in Illinois. When she started having pains, Robert found a house off the main road. An older couple opened their home, and she delivered a healthy baby girl that night. This was a normal situation on the pioneer road west.

December 24, 1837
I cannot sleep because I am so happy to have our family together for Christmas. We agreed that, except for Charles and baby Helen, there would be no gifts. Having our family together and a new baby, how could we possibly ask God for more? Robert's eyes sparkled like a child tonight when he saw his father cut the apple and read from the family Bible, just as he had done for as long as Robert could remember. I know he will keep his father's tradition in his family. We are blessed.

December 24, 1837

The unexpected early arrival of Robert and Jane Ann was celebrated with a new baby. Jane Ann was glad to have her Mama to teach her to care for baby Helen. Thomas was proud to have his son working with him in his law office. He needed the help, and Robert was quickly accepted in the community. Thomas L. was mentoring with the local wheelwright, learning to make wagon wheels, and Thomas helped him refine his woodworking skills. By Christmas, everyone had settled into life in Missouri.

February 19, 1838

I am so proud Robert and Thomas are working on the legal documents to incorporate our growing town. Robert has gained the people's confidence and earned their trust. He has been asked to serve as one of the first trustees for Springfield. He is honored and will do a good job.

Soon, homestead land will be available in the next county. Before it does, we will move there and establish ourselves like we did here. Thomas will pick the exact land he thinks is best for apple orchards, and hopefully we will be settled by Christmas.

Last week for Charles's seventh birthday we had a snowball fight and made snow cream.

February 19, 1838

Robert could have been a lawyer in Cincinnati, but instead he chose to practice law with his father in Springfield. He was soon asked to be a circuit lawyer and traveled from town to town by horseback. Always known as a man with deep faith in God, he was respected by the courts.

Summer 1838

Before we started that morning, we prayed, "Be the good Lord willing and the creeks don't rise." We did not turn back. We made it past Turn Back Creek and on to Mount Vernon, where land will open for homesteading next year. We will stay in our covered wagon until we find a cabin to get us by through winter. Thomas has walked through many fields and now knows which land will be best for us. He has drawn the plans for our house, a barn, and an apple orchard. When the land is ours, Robert and Thomas L. will help us build a one-room cabin to live in until our home is built.

It has been six years since I told Thomas I would agree to go west. A long hard road we have traveled to get here. I can tell Thomas is tired and he needs more rest. He reminds me often that we are almost home.

Summer 1838

Thomas did not tell Frances he hadn't been feeling well for a long time. At fifty-six years old, the travel and the harsh winters had finally taken a toll on him.

September 16, 1838

My heart is shattered and my hand shakes to think I must write these words in our family Bible.

Thomas Crawford

Born 1782

Died September 16, 1838

Mount Vernon, Missouri

September 16, 1838

Always before dawn, Thomas was awake, sitting in the cane-bottom chair by the fire.

The first thing Frances saw when she woke each morning was the silhouette of the man she loved, waiting for her by the warm fire.

On this day when she got up, he wasn't there. Thinking perhaps she'd overslept, she threw the patchwork quilt to the side and started to stand up. Over her shoulder, she saw him. He didn't move and didn't say a word. She knew what had happened, and her heart sank in unbearable pain. Thomas had died during the night.

Walking slowly to his bedside, she stood looking at Thomas, hoping deep in her soul that he would look up at her and smile. Pulling the cane chair from near the fireplace, she sat down beside him. She picked up his lifeless hand, rubbed it against her face, and kissed his forehead. Tears fell from her eyes onto his face. She kept holding his hand as she laid her head on the down-filled bed. Her flowing tears ran down his hand and onto his arm. Trying not to wake up Thomas L. and Charles, she sat beside him, with only the dim light from the fading fire.

Memories danced in her mind while she stared at his handsome face that no longer looked up at her with his gentle smile.

Thomas L. stirred as he started to wake up. Without a word, she raised her head and gave him a glance.

The dawn barely breaking gave enough light through the window for him to see the glistening tears on his mother's face. He knew what had happened. He got up, walked over near her, and bowed beside the bed. Laying his head on the bed, he cried. Frances softly rubbed his back as she kept holding Thomas's hand.

Hearing Charles wakening, Thomas L. went to sit beside him on the bed to tell him his Papa had died. His young eight-year-old heart suddenly experienced the deep pain from his Papa's death.

Without being asked, Thomas L. went to get Mr. Fulbright and the doctor. He then saddled his horse and rode to Springfield to tell Robert and Jane Ann. Getting there as soon as they could, Robert made all the arrangements and got permission for their father to be buried at the Neely Cemetery. Thomas went back to be at his mother's side.

The night after Thomas's funeral, Frances couldn't sleep. She was not at peace in her grief. And she knew what she had to do. Pushing the covers away, she got down on her knees on the hard-splintered floor. With all her strength, she said, "I thank you, heavenly Father, for another day that has come and gone."

Much time and many tears passed before Frances could thank God for another "good" day.

Late Fall 1838

Thomas L. is only twenty- one years old and feels he is now responsible for Charles and me. He loved Thomas so much and would do anything to care for us. But I hope he will make his own way and find what God has called him to do in his life. Somehow, we will get through the days ahead.

Fall 1838

Thomas L. had gone into Springfield to pick up supplies to prepare for winter. As he started back to Mount Vernon, soldiers on horseback blocked the road. Behind them were Indian families walking. Their faces were so sad. The Indians had been forced from their homes by the Indian Removal act and forced to move their families to the Indian Territory the U S Government had established for them.

Thomas L. and others watched the Indians cry as they walked. Some people said the Indians cried because they had to give up their land. Others said the people who saw them cried with them. Their path was called, "The Trail of Tears."

Thomas L. never got over seeing the sadness of the Indians. From that day on, his heart was broken for the Indians.

September 12, 1839

Celebration day finally has arrived. We were first in line to file our claim. Standing by my side, Thomas L. and Charles watched as I signed my name, Frances Catts Crawford. I thought about Thomas, and oh, how I wished he could have been with us. We sang all the way from town to our new home. The boys followed on their horses, whooping and hollering all the way.

I pulled our wagon onto our land. Our land. With confidence, I stood up and shouted, "In God has been our trust!" With joy in my heart, I climbed down from the wagon. As a surprise, I had made a kite. Thomas tied it to his saddle horn and rode Charles through the fields with the kite flying high above. I began to walk. Finding each post that marked our land, I walked and prayed from one to the other.

Meeting the boys back at the wagon, we held hands and started to pray. Hearing a noise, we stopped. In their wagon, here came Robert, Jane Ann, and baby Helen.

Behind them came the Fulbrights and the Williamses. They circled with us to pray, and to dedicate the land to God. Knowing we wanted to sleep in our covered wagon tonight on our land, Jane Ann brought us a new crazy quilt she had made from fabric scraps. She embroidered a briar-stitch between the fabric pieces.

Robert gave Thomas L. a new saw and an ax. Charles, waiting to see what he would be given, was handed a shovel and a hammer. The Fulbrights had a picnic with plenty extra for supper. The Williamses brought a goat to chew away the brush. Friends are coming on Saturday to help build us a cabin to stay in for winter. Until then, we will be happy in our covered wagon.

Thomas L. wants to sleep in the possum belly under the wagon to keep watch through the night. We no longer must gather wood for a fire along our way. Tonight, thank you, Lord, we are home.

Thomas has been on my heart all day. I'm not sure what happens in heaven, but I feel him watching over us.

September 12, 1839

Homesteading day arrived. Before sunup, Mount Vernon bustled with activity. Flickering lanterns guided people as they ran to get in line at the land office.

Frances Catts Crawford was first in line with her boys, Thomas L. and Charles. Waiting all night in the dark on the porch with her sleeping boys leaning against her, Frances thought about all the things that had happened along their journey to finally come to this day.

Dozing on and off, she thought about Thomas's smile when she told him she would go west. And how proud he was when he showed her where he put the carved sign on their wagon with the beloved words from her friend's poem.

The road they'd traveled since they left Virginia in 1834 had been long and hard.

Hearing sounds inside the land office, Frances struggled to wake up. Behind her, people anxiously waited to file a claim for the rich farm land around Mount Vernon.

The door suddenly opened, and Frances stepped forward. Today she would fulfill Thomas's dream.

Her son, Robert, excused his way into the land office to be her lawyer if needed as she filed her claim to the land. She walked out with her claim papers held high. The people in line cheered, hoping they too would have their claim soon filed.

Frances's wagon was already filled with supplies and the mules harnessed and ready to go. Driving her team of mules south out of town with the boys following behind on their horses, she soon pulled the wagon onto their land. She danced her feet back and forth across the sign attached to the buckboard. Finally, they were home.

Before leaving, Robert handed his mother a letter from George.

Frances read, "Dear Mama, I am getting married."

Spring 1840

I am not sure who planned it or how word got out there would be a barn raising at the Catts/Crawford farm. I think Charles might have had something to do with it. It seems the preacher had many questions for him and Thomas L. after church last Sunday. But we are thankful to all our good neighbors and friends who came in wagons and by horseback to build the barn in just one day.

The women brought food, watched after the children, and kept the men organized. I saw one woman carry at least a dozen buckets filled with nails to the men. They carried them water and lemonade too.

He was late getting here, but Robert was soon up on top hammering nails with the other men. It was a community effort to help us build our barn. Every day I am more thankful for the place we live.

Charles has been getting in trouble for sneaking away to swim in the cold water in Honey Creek. I caught him before he and the boys from town slipped away through the woods. I asked Thomas L. to keep an eye on the boys while he worked on the barn roof. They tried, but they did not get away.

Spring 1840

People were glad Frances and her family decided to stay. Neighbors helped neighbors. When Frances received money from last year's apple crop in Virginia, she loaned money to those in the community who needed it. Grateful for her kindness, those who borrowed from her paid back with interest.

Late Summer 1840

I did not look at the date on George's letter that Robert delivered to me on the day we claimed our land. While we were trying to get settled, build a cabin before winter and a shed for the animals, I did not have time to write him. Today I received a letter signed "George and Mary Ann." They informed me that their new baby girl was named after her mother, Mary Ann, and me, Frances. They named her Mary Frances and will call her Fannie. She was born on May 10, 1840. I sat pondering what I was reading, realizing I had never heard about Mary Ann.

I found the letter from George and reread it. I hadn't noticed it was dated January 15, 1839. It must have been lost and later delivered to Robert after we left Springfield. And I did not notice on the bottom of the letter that George had written, "We are getting married on February 1, Mary Ann's birthday."

Feeling so bad I had not known George was married for over a year, I sat down right then and wrote George and Mary Ann a letter. I later asked Robert and Jane Ann if they knew about George's wedding. They had known all about the wedding and assumed I knew also. Jane Ann made a quilt for baby Fannie and sent it with a family traveling to Virginia. So, I guess mamas are always the last to know!

Late Summer 1840

Mary Ann Tarr was strikingly beautiful. Her long brown hair, brown eyes, and sweet smile caught George Catts's attention the day she came into the mercantile where he worked. Within a short time, they fell in love.

Known as an excellent woodworker, George made Mary Ann a Virginia cherrywood keepsake box. On the top of the box, in the beautiful cherrywood grain, he carved a big heart and inside it, he carved, "To my sweet Mary Ann." On the corner of the box, he carved their initials and under those, in scrolled letters, he carved, "Forever."

Her mother was from the Perry family, who all served in the Navy. George wanted to properly propose to Mary Ann and went to her father and asked for his blessing to marry his daughter. He refused because George was not from a military family.

They eloped on her birthday, February 1, 1839, and her family disowned her. Hurt by her family's response, they soon started their own family. George and Mary Ann were called a "True Love Story."

Frances reminded George he said he would move to Missouri after he found his bride.

February 14, 1841

Charles was happy today, his tenth birthday. After a good church service, I was delighted our family could celebrate his big day together. I think Charles ate more cake than anyone. I wish George and his family could have been with us since his birthday is the day before Charles's. I sent a pack to him a month ago, but I have not yet heard if he received it or not. I reminded him that he hoped to move to Missouri after he found his bride.

Thomas would be proud of his son, Charles. He has a kind heart and loves animals. I do worry about his strong will. I pray he will use it to be a good man and not let it bring him harm. Thomas's death when he was only seven has left an empty spot in his heart that I cannot fill. I am thankful Thomas L. is teaching him manly ways and that Robert spends time with him teaching him integrity and honesty.

Tonight, I will thank God for another very good day with family.

February 14, 1841

Over two years had gone by since Thomas Crawford died. The family did well to settle into Mount Vernon and make it home. The farm kept Frances, Thomas L., and Charles busy without much time for play. A family party was a good break for everyone.

December 6, 1841

Christmas will be in our new home. Not everything is finished, but the roof is on, walls are up, and enough firewood to get us through winter is stacked. It has been a long time it seems since I have been able to appreciate my family. Thomas L. has cut trees for two years to build our house and the barn. I am certain he feels responsible to care for me since Thomas died. I wish he would start his own life and a family. Charles likes to help Thomas L., but I insist he does his schoolwork first. If he had his way, he would never learn to read or write. He would rather care for horses and cows.

Robert, Jane Ann, and the three children will be here soon for a surprise party for Thomas L.. Robert has a huge surprise for him. A businessman in Springfield needed Robert to represent him in court but afterward could not pay him. He raises horses. Rather than owe Robert, he wants him to have one of his best horses as payment. Knowing all Thomas has done for his Mama, Robert wants Thomas L. to have the horse. The fine horse has been broken but will still need work. Winter is not the best time to work with a new animal, but Thomas L. will enjoy the challenge and be proud to have him.

To show my love and appreciation for all the work Thomas L. has done, I will give him money to buy a new saddle. Jane Ann has never sewn a leather skin before. She hopes her brother will like the wide-brimmed hat she made for him. George sent money to purchase a hunting knife for his brother Thomas L., and Charles has secretly worked for weeks to make him a leather sheath for the knife. He had Mr. Moore help him carve T. L. C., across the top. Neighbors and friends are coming to celebrate. His cake is hidden under a dishpan on the back porch until the party begins. Robert has promised he will dunk Charles in the icy rain barrel if he has told Thomas about the party.

December 1841

After Thomas died, Thomas L. was sad the father he loved so much and had made him feel like his own son suddenly was gone. Unable to take time to grieve, he silently held his pain. He worked hard to care for his mother after she got the land. His brothers knew Thomas L. deserved their gratitude. And now it was his turn to be honored.

March 1842

Robert has become a well-respected lawyer in Springfield and as the circuit court attorney. His father, Thomas Crawford, and his uncle, Charles Hammond, had always taught him to be respectful to the courts and the judges at all times and under all circumstances. Jane Ann told me that Robert had disagreed with a poor decision a judge made and felt that the judge had hurt the lives of the families involved.

He had said, "Respectfully, Your Honor, I disagree. I cannot leave the courtroom without saying, sir, there is only one God that judges a man's soul as to the reasons for his deeds, and you, sir, are not him."

Since Robert is in court most often in Springfield, he has purchased them a small house in town. They will share their time between Springfield and Mount Vernon.

The winds and spring rains have started early. I have learned to watch the chickens and the other animals as well as the skies, to see when a storm is coming. Thomas cleaned out the snake skins from the cellar and has it ready to use.

Charles thought it was funny to lay the snake skins on the porch for me to see. I responded to his ornery prank, "Only six this year. Last year there were seven."

Charles decided he would try to bait skunks near the edge of the woods to keep them away from the house. He was skunked by the first one he caught. I was upset with him that I had to use my good canned tomatoes to pour on him to remove the skunk smell. And his clothes had to be buried in the garden for a week. I insisted he dig up his muddy-smelly clothes and wash them himself. He has not said another word about trying to catch a skunk.

March 1842

Robert was away more as circuit attorney for the courts, and Jane Ann accepted her responsibilities as best she could. They had four little ones and another on the way. Their son, Joel, insisted he will be a doctor, not a lawyer.

Frances and her sons have adjusted well to farm life. She often tried not to show she was afraid so Charles and Thomas L. wouldn't laugh at her. She took one day at a time in learning to live on the farm.

January 1843

My beloved friend has died. On his way to court in the next county on horseback, Robert stopped to bring me a newspaper from Springfield. On the front page in bold letters was written, "Francis Scott Key, Author of the Star-Spangled Banner, died in Baltimore, Maryland, January 11, 1843."

I had to sit down on the porch in shock. The air was cold, but I don't think I could feel it. I first thought about Ms. Polly and their eleven children. For as long as I could remember, I had known Frankie. As a little girl, he entertained me while our parents talked politics and war. I was the bothersome little child that he was always kind to when our families got together. He would read poetry and act out Shakespeare for me. As a little girl, I looked up to him and loved him like a brother. When he married Polly, I remember he danced with me at their wedding, and we promised to be friends forever. He and Polly came to my wedding to John and when John was injured at Fort McHenry.

I will never forget when we walked together in our rose garden, and he read to me the poem he wrote when he saw the flag over the fort still standing. I smile every time I hear someone sing, The Star-Spangled Banner. I thought about the poet writer's society that Frankie and my brother, John Neal, established in Baltimore and the poems they wrote.

When I moved to Virginia to marry Thomas, Frankie and his family came to Baltimore to tell me goodbye. Ms. Polly wrote every Christmas to tell me how they were doing. I loved him as a dear friend and he loved me.

I wrote a letter to Polly but am not sure how long it will take to get delivered to her. A month after he died, she wrote me a letter telling me how much they both loved me and missed me after we moved west. She said he died from pleurisy at their daughter,

Elizabeth's, house in Baltimore. She said he was sixty-three years old. To me, he will always be young Frankie.

Thomas came up from the barn and insisted I go inside by the warm fire. When I told him Frankie had died, he took the worn, wooden board down from the mantel and laid it in my lap. Then he handed me the box containing the piece of the flag and made me some hot tea. He respectfully left me alone with my memories.

January 1843

America grieved for the man who made the American flag respectfully famous.

July 1843

We have the biggest and the best garden I have ever seen. We are supplying all our neighbors with food. Charles and Thomas L. have dug us a deep cellar to store our winter foods. I build a fire out back most every day to boil my canning jars and to seal them tight. Canned green beans and tomatoes will make good stew in winter, and peaches and apples for a cobbler will be a special treat for Thanksgiving. I think we will have an abundance of black walnuts and pecans for pies and candy if the squirrels will stay away.

I guess I never thought about the hard work we would do once we homesteaded the farm. There seems to be endless work and longer days than I would have ever imagined. And so many things I had never heard before. An old man stopped by last week to see if I had any cackleberries he might could have. Never having heard of them, I said no.

He replied, "Well, you've got chickens, ain't ya?" I now know that he was asking for some eggs.

Robert was elected Circuit Attorney Pro Tem and will need to travel to several counties for court. He was given a saddle bag with his name on it from the courts to carry his legal papers. Jane Ann is concerned that he is sometimes too outspoken. Last week he and another attorney got in a fight during court. The judge fined them both ten dollars.

Thomas has been telling me about the wagon trains that go west to California. People meet in Independence Missouri, north from us, with their covered wagon ready to travel. They sign up to travel with a Wagon Master who has experience traveling the trail. He does not think people know how hard the trail west will be. He *said our one-thousand-mile trip from Virginia to Missouri was hard enough, but the trip west will be two-thousand miles over prairies and mountains.*

I remember I once said that I hoped I would not have need to visit or live in Missouri. Oh, how life changes. For me, I think Missouri is where I will stay.

July 1843

Over one thousand settlers pulled out from Independence, Missouri, on May 22, 1842, headed for Oregon, part of what was called the Great Migration west. Newspapers ran stories about how wonderful California and Oregon would be, free land and sunshine all year long. People imagined life would be so wonderful that a mindset to go west became common. They heard over and over again, "Go west young man, go west." Very few stories were written about the challenges and heartache on the trail. Or how many did not survive to see the land of sunshine.

Summer 1844

I am so proud of our home and farm place. I wish Thomas could sit here beside me on the porch and see all that has been accomplished because of his dream to go west. He would enjoy listening to the whippoorwills and crickets just before the sun goes down. It is a restful place I call home.

But it does have challenges. A snake has been getting in the hen house and is eating the eggs. I solved the problem by putting hard-boiled duck eggs in the chicken's nests. I outsmarted the snake. When he ate the hard-boiled egg, he died. Thomas found him in the field beyond the chicken house.

I may have been born in the city, but I have adjusted quite well to farm life. There is one thing from my city life that I hope to one day have on the farm. His and hers outhouses.

I will not be surprised if Thomas L. leaves to go with a wagon train west in the spring. He talks about it so much, I know it is his heart to go. If that is what he wants, I want it also, I tell myself.

Summer 1844

Frances came from the big city of Baltimore. Her sister Rachel and her brother John Neal would be amazed to see her so well adjusted to farm life.

April 1, 1845

I stood in the road and watched Thomas L. ride away. I made sure he saw me smiling, not crying when he left. I waited to see if he would turn around and come back home. I am glad he did not. Now my tears can fall. As much as I will miss him, I am glad he is starting his own life. He has cared for Charles and me since the morning Thomas died. He built the house, the barn, the cellar, the chicken house, our cabin, and two outhouses—his and hers. He and Charles have cut enough firewood for five years. The fields and garden are ready for planting, and the animals are healthy. He even made new wagon wheels for our wagon. Since that is what he will be doing on the wagon train, he wanted us to have his best work.

Last night I gave him a Bible. While writing his name in the front of the Bible, I prayed for God's protective hand to be with him and for him to come home safely. Jane Ann gave him a diary and trail maps. Charles made sure he had his hunting knife and food, hardtack, and beef jerky. Robert was glad he has the good horse to ride on the trail west and apple seeds in his pocket.

Before climbing on his horse, Thomas L. gave me a hug and whispered, "I left you a gift, Mama. But you have to find it." Then he climbed up in his saddle and was ready to go. Smiling, he leaned down and rubbed Charles's head, and reminded him that he promised not to tell.

I reached up and held his hand tight and told him once more that I loved him.

He squeezed my hand and rode away.

April 1, 1845

Thomas L. needed the Oregon Trail as much as the trail needed him. He was a good wheelwright and would be needed by many families on the difficult trails west. But Thomas L. needed to find himself and discover the man God intended him become. The Indians had been on his heart since he saw the Trail of Tears go through Springfield years before. Thomas later said he felt God's call for him to take Scriptures to the Indians.

May 18, 1845

Since Thomas L. loved long walks in the woods and watching the animals, I thought that perhaps that might be where I would find the gift he left for me to find. Shortly after he left, I started taking walks in the woods by myself. I needed the time alone to pray for our family.

As I was walking early one morning, I discovered the May apples

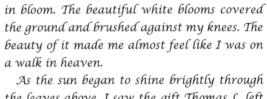

in bloom. The beautiful white blooms covered the ground and brushed against my knees. The beauty of it made me almost feel like I was on a walk in heaven.

As the sun began to shine brightly through the leaves above, I saw the gift Thomas L. left for me to find. He had carved a cross on to the stump of a tree. As I got closer, the sunlight from above illuminated the cross. I bowed down and prayed for my son on his way west

Thomas always had a way of touching my heart after little Clarence died. I know I shall spend many days walking to the cross in the woods.

July 1845

I got a letter from Thomas L. that was two months old when I received it. He said he is doing well and learning the trail. He wishes Charles and I could see the open prairies with herds of buffalo roaming wild and the beauty of the mountains. But the mountains were the most difficult part of the trip so far. He said at times they must use pulleys to pull the wagons up one side of the mountain and to lower them down the other side. And he said that it is hard work beyond what he had imagined. Charles and I miss him so much but are happy he has finally found what he wants in life. Charles complains about having to do more work since Thomas L. is gone.

Charles and I will go to the celebration in town for Independence Day. I think every person in the county is planning on attending.

July 1845

The entire county came to celebrate Independence Day, and they were excited to celebrate Mount Vernon being established as the new county seat. Every citizen in Mount Vernon made an effort to be part of the barbecue and barn dance. Oxen, sheep, pigs, and other animals were roasted and served with a dish of the best recipe from every family.

Trees had been cut and brush cleared away. A plot of ground was cleared and leveled smooth. Two inches of wheat bran was scattered all over the flat ground and was declared to be the "Mount Vernon Ball Room" for the night.

Music was provided by a single violinist who could play only two songs, "Rye Straw" and "Chicken Pie."

"He alternated playing the two songs until he plum wore out," the newspaper stated.

Always willing to do her part, Frances Crawford kindly donated the sugar to make candy for the children.

March 1846

Thomas L. has told us so many stories about the west. Many things that I had no idea existed. He once helped a couple who had an orphan wagon for children they were trying to find a home for. Their parents had been killed or they had been abandoned in Independence, Missouri.

An older couple had been feeding the street children and tried to find them a home. They decided they wanted to go west, and since no one would take the children, they took them with them hoping to find a home along the way to California. They started by asking the families on the wagon train if they would take one of the children. At every town they asked if there was anyone who would take the children. No one would take them so Thomas asked the families if they would help the older couple feed the children. Slowly, the families learned to love the children, and by the time they reached Oregon, all of the children had homes.

I know God has placed my soft-hearted Thomas on the trail for such a time as this.

March 1846

Frances loved having Thomas home and to hear the stories about his travels. She knew time was getting close for him to leave again. Her prayers always went before him on the trail.

Christmas 1847

We are together for Christmas, and that is all that matters. Thomas is home from the trail, and Robert has put aside his work until after Christmas Day. Jane Ann and their four children came out early to help me cook. Charles is helping the little ones decorate the pine tree Thomas L. cut for them. He bought special gifts in California for us all this year. Last year he brought me a brush, comb, and mirror set with painted lavender flowers. He is the one that remembers I like pretty lavender things.

Jane Ann loves sewing for us all. I still have the pretty pink hat she made for me for my birthday after John Neal died. She has such a heart with compassion. I bought her a nice pair of black gloves and have embroidered her initials on them, J. A. C., in shiny black thread. And I will give her my locket with her father's picture inside.

I wanted just a moment to write in my journal while I have a cup of hot tea before the Christmas activities begin. I love to look at the wooden sign that hangs above the fireplace. My dear husband John carved those words as my Christmas gift while he was in pain from his shrapnel wounds. He had no idea the journey his sign would go on nor the comfort the words would give to me.

And Thomas, who made the sign into a step on the buckboard on our wagon, had no idea the confidence the words would give me when I homesteaded this land. With the uncertainties life gives each day, I still hold on to those faithful words, "In God is our trust."

Thank you again, John, for the best Christmas gift ever.

April 1, 1848

Thomas received a letter from his wagon master asking him to come early to help prepare for the wagons to roll west. He wrote that gold had been discovered in California and that so many people wanted to go west he needed his help as soon as he could get to Independence.

I am hurrying to help him pack for the trail. I will spend the afternoon finishing the coat I have been working on all winter for him. I am sad to see him go early, and when Charles gets home from school, he will be disappointed. There is no time to go to Springfield to let Robert and Jane Ann know he is leaving. As with every year, I will hold my tears until he is gone.

1848

Word spread quickly. "There's gold in them there hills." Gold had been discovered in the race of an old water mill in California. People fought to buy wagons in Independence, Missouri, so they could make the two-thousand-mile trip in hopes of finding gold. The Oregon Trail was widened in 1848 to make room for the thousands of settlers going west for a new reason.

November 1849

Thomas has ridden on the Oregon Trail for five years, and he has finally been named a scout by the wagon master. Five years it has taken for the Indians to recognize him as a friend. He said he knows the trail, yet it is ever changing. One year it is in a drought, the next year, flooding. He said that people are the most unpredictable and are why he loves the trail.

He thinks the California Gold Rush has created a new breed of settlers that have only one thing on their minds—gold. They call themselves, "The 49ers." They race past families on the trail, trying to be first to get to the gold. Their greed is fueling the fires of lawlessness. Thomas said his devotion is not to the gold rushers but remains with the Indians and the families whose dreams are to go west for a better life.

November 1849

The California Gold Rush populated most of California in less than a year. The lust for gold caused the worst to come out in some people. Claim jumping, greed, and robbery were the result of their uncontrollable desire for more gold. California, the land of sunshine also became the land of robbers and thieves.

Spring 1850

I received a belated birthday letter from George and Mary Ann. He wanted me to know he is considering moving his bride to Missouri. And that he had never forgotten what he told me fifteen years ago on the last day he saw me in Virginia.

Spring 1850

George has sold his mercantile in Virginia and is preparing for a move to Missouri. He has worked with his Crawford brothers in the apple orchards to assure everything is in order for him to leave Virginia next year.

February 1, 1851

George has not written to tell me when they will move to Missouri. He tells me he has many things to take care of before he can make a move. Jane Ann said Mary Ann is expecting and had been having a very difficult pregnancy. I pray for her and my entire family. But her baby has been on my heart in recent weeks. I look forward to meeting Mary Ann, the new baby, and the other children. And oh, how much I have missed George over the many years since we said goodbye. Never would I have imagined it would be so long before I would see my son again. If I knew when, I would count the days until they arrive.

Robert is very active in the community. He is a leader in his lodge and has a plan to build houses for new people coming to Mount Vernon. He is always thinking ahead and sometimes does not slow down to enjoy today.

Christmas 1851

Christmas is my most special time of year. I love everything about it but most of all, our family being together. But it seems different this year. Everyone else is doing what I have always done. Robert and Jane Ann tell me I should rest.

Since Thomas L. came home from the trail, he works in the barn most all day, and he won't let me see what he is working on. Perhaps it is Christmas gifts, but he always brings presents from California.

Charles has been tying garland together all week. He said he has the perfect tree already picked out to cut and will help the little children decorate.

Jane Ann has the meal planned. She has already dipped pine cones in paraffin wax for the table and mantel. She told me I should rest and crochet a new lace table cloth to use on Christmas Eve. I feel so useless. I am not yet sixty, so I can't imagine why I am being treated this way. I am not sick or suffer from broken bones. Perhaps I should stand on a chair in the kitchen and yell, "Why am I being treated this way?" And remind them, "I am your Mother."

They told me we might have a long evening and that I just needed to rest. Light snow had been falling all day. It looked like shinning sugar on white cake icing. Charles went outside to hang garland and red berries around the porch post while the little ones watched from the window. Then he came inside, and he let them hang garland on the mantel above the fireplace and decorate the tree. He was careful with the wooden sign and my box that contained the flag. Robert was helping Jane Ann in the kitchen, and I could tell they were almost finished preparing our Christmas Eve supper.

I heard a wagon outside and voices, then a knock on the door. Smiling, Robert said, "You should go to the door, Mama." I could hear giggles and whispering outside. I opened the door, and there stood my son George and his family! I had not seen his face in seventeen years. George helped his sweet Mary Ann inside and got her close to the fire so she could warm up. She unwrapped her coat, and I saw little Clarence for the first time. The other children gave me a hug as they told me their names.

I could not stop hugging on George and my family I had never met. After we finished the best Christmas supper ever, we moved over to sit by the fire. It was time for the story about the star over Bethlehem the night Jesus was born.  Thomas taught all the boys how to slice open the apple to see the star. Thomas L. had told the story last year. He handed the apple and the knife to Charles and said, "It is your turn, little brother."

Afterward we waited for Robert to read from the family Bible. Instead, he handed the Bible to George and said, "It is your turn."

How could I ask God for more than these moments?

Thomas and Charles must have slipped out the back door to the barn. I heard a commotion in front of the house. Again, Robert said, "You need to open the door, Mama."

As I reached for the door, I heard bells jingling. When I opened the door, I saw the most beautiful horse-drawn sleigh, with swags of berries and garland, two big red bows, and oil lanterns on each side.

Everyone yelled, "Merry Christmas!"

I did not have time to cry before they loaded me and all the grandchildren into the sleigh. Jane Ann had warmed blankets to put over us and had new hats and mittens for each child. Everyone but Mary Ann and baby Clarence went out for a ride. Thomas drove the horse while everyone took turns riding through the snow-covered fields at night in our new sleigh. Across the back of the sleigh, Thomas had painted a red sign, "The Catts/Crawford Family."

I sat by the fire with Mary Ann for a long time and held baby Clarence so she could rest.

I will count my blessings tonight and thank God for another good Christmas with my family.

Thomas said he will have the sleigh ready for rides after Christmas morning breakfast.

Christmas 1851

The Catts/Crawford family had the Merriest Christmas ever. George and his family had been at Robert and Jane Ann's house in Springfield for a week, planning the Christmas Eve surprise for their mother.

Spring 1852

George and Mary Ann are settled in their house on the corner of Cherry and Hazel in town. Today George will open the first mercantile in our town. He has decided to name it, "Mount Vernon Mercantile." The name will make people feel it is their new store also. To celebrate, he is having a five-cent sale. Muslin fabric will be five cents a yard, nails, five cents per pound and bacon, five cents a pound. He said he would have something for everyone.

Having owned the mercantile back home, he knows pricing and procurement. He ordered the stock for the store before he left Virginia. Robert found the building for him and is advising him on legal matters. Jane Ann came last week to clean and organize the shelves, so they are ready for his merchandise. Charles and the little children hope candy sticks will be free for family.

Mary Ann has not gained her strength back after the long and difficult move from Virginia. She and little Clarence rest and stay inside most days. He is such a sweet and loving child. When George sees Mary Ann and Clarence coming down the street, he smiles so big. He and Mary Ann are so much in love. I am thankful I can help with little Clarence so she can rest. I pray they will both have better days ahead.

Thomas L. left last month to go on the yearly wagon train. He continues to be on my heart the last few weeks. Charles would like to go with him someday, but I think most likely he will have horses and cattle in his future.

I wake up praying for our family, and I go to bed praying for them. I do thank God for another good day when I am with my family.

Spring 1852

The trip was so hard on Mary Ann and little Clarence. She was frail, and he was tiny. All the family was concerned about them. Whatever they needed, the family jumped in to help. Robert went to help George unpack crates at the mercantile. He cut his hand on the wood. They laughed about when they cut their thumbs to become blood brothers. They have always been close and will need to be in the future.

Christmas 1852

I am so happy to have a houseful for Christmas Eve dinner. George is here and is doing well with his mercantile in town. Mary Ann and little Clarence are some better. They came out earlier today so they would not have to be out in the cold night air.

Thomas L. is home and always has exciting stories to tell about his friends, the Indians. I can tell he is getting weary after traveling now for seven years on the Oregon Trail. Charles misses him so much and sits for hours listening to his stories.

Robert, Jane Ann, and their eight children will be here soon. We will all be together for Christmas morning.

Thomas L. tells us he uses apples to tell the Indians the story about the star over Bethlehem just like Papa Crawford taught him. And he showed us the apple seed box where he keeps the seeds that he plants along the trail.

Robert has told the apple story since his father passed away, then Thomas and now, Charles. Since George and his family are with *us, George will read from the family Bible. After we sing together, Jane Ann will ask the children to close their eyes and see if they get a surprise. Charles will put candy under each chair. It is the little things we will remember most about our Christmas's together.*

I sit in the corner, quiet as a mouse, listening to their laughter and watching them have a good time together. I feel so blessed to have our family home for Christmas.

Christmas 1852

Christmas always meant the birth of Jesus to the Catts/ Crawford family. But Frances also loved to read a special story to her grandchildren after they hung up their stockings. She would begin, "'Twas the night before Christmas and all through the house, not a creature was stirring, not ever a mouse ...."

Thanksgiving 1853

Charles, now twenty-two, was proud he shot our big Thanksgiving turkey. He said his turkey is so big, he has earned the right to brag about it.

Little Clarence does not need to be out in the cold, so we have decided to take our Thanksgiving feast to him. Thomas came up with the idea. If George will let us all come to their house, he must see to it that sweet Mary Ann does not cook anything. He agreed, and we made our plans.

Thomas and Charles will cook the turkey, roasted yams, and Indian corn soup. The granddaughters will help me make the cornbread dressing, winter mashed potatoes, and pumpkin pies. The boys can help Robert chop two loads of firewood to take to George. One for his house and one for the wood stove in the mercantile. Jane Ann will do all the finishing touches, including bring Mary Ann a new winter-white crocheted shawl to keep her warm. And for tiny little Clarence, she will make a blue sweater and hat to keep him warm. All that would be missing would be their daughter, Fannie, who was back east at the girl's academy.

Unknown to us all, Thomas brought home a new chocolate candy called Ghirardelli Chocolates from San Francisco. So excited, but so stuffed from our Thanksgiving meal, we still ate our chocolates.

I am grateful for the caring, loving hearts in our family.

Thanksgiving 1853

The Catts/Crawford family was thankful to gather together and were thankful for the Lord's blessings.

Mary Ann received a letter from her cousin, telling her that her uncle, Commodore Matthew Perry—Mary Ann's uncle— had successfully taken a steamship across the ocean to a country called Japan. He negotiated with Japan to open their country for trade with the United States.

February 1, 1854

Today, we are going to celebrate two birthdays. Little Clarence was born on his Mama's birthday. He is three years old, and I am not certain about Mary Ann's age. Her cake is baked, and I have a small one for him. Charles, Thomas L., and I are loaded and ready to go to their house in town. The snow is deep, but I feel we can't miss little Clarence's birthday. He is in bed so much of the time, so I just want to be there to see him happy if only for a little while. If they can get through the snow, Jane Ann and family will meet us there. I am thankful Thomas is with us in case we get stuck. I have a bag packed in case we get snowed in, in town.

George showed me the china music box he ordered for Mary Ann's birthday. It has a pink rose painted on the top and plays the song, "Mary Had a Little Lamb." He thinks the song was written for her and little Clarence. Before we go out to get in the wagon, I will sit here by the fire to warm my feet for just a little while longer. And I will pray for God to be with us in the days ahead.

February 1, 1854

The doctor had been by to see little Clarence and told George he's not doing well at all. He'd try a new medicine to help with his breathing, but there wasn't much he could do. The doctor thought that because Clarence was premature, his lungs weren't fully developed when he was born. The family realized what was ahead and made every effort to be with him on his birthday.

April 16, 1854

We have been taking turns sitting with little Clarence throughout the night. His fever is still high, and his breathing is shallow. We all gathered around his bed and sang praise songs over him and prayed. When Mary Ann sat down beside him on his bed, he opened his eyes and smiled at his Mama. Tears ran down her face. Little Clarence reached his tiny frail hand up and wiped his Mama's tears away. Then he closed his eyes.

We left Mary Ann and George alone to be with little Clarence. We could hear them crying. The church bells began to ring at ten o'clock for the Easter Sunday services. Sweet William, Clarence's brother, said that was an angel ringing the bells to let us know he made it to heaven.

Every heart in our family hurt the day that our little Clarence died.

George had already shown Thomas L. and Robert where he would like Clarence buried on the farm. Charles and Robert went to dig the grave. Thankful he had not yet left to go with the wagon train, Thomas L. went to the barn to build the casket. Jane Ann had already sewn a little suit for Clarence, so she helped Thomas L. line the small casket with white velvet. I went home to make a soft pillow for sweet Clarence to rest his head on in the casket. I pulled the down feathers from my pillow to stuff the white satin pillow for him.

George later told me that when little Clarence was being taken away, the china music box on the oak dresser started playing, "Mary Had a Little Lamb."

Only God could comfort our broken hearts.

April 16, 1854, Easter Sunday

Little Clarence was the first buried in the Catts/Crawford Cemetery. George made a cross for his son's grave. Mary Ann would never get over losing little Clarence.

Early Spring 1855

The wagons rolled west this year without Thomas L. He traveled the trail for ten years. The first two years he was a wheelwright, making and repairing wagon wheels. The following year the wagon master asked him to ride with his scout to learn the skills to become a scout. This pleased Thomas L. because that was why he went on the Oregon Trail. He explained to me that the scout is one who builds a friendship with the Indians so the wagons will be able to peacefully pass through their land. He tells me that he gradually gained their trust and learned their language. He then taught them his language. With communication, he would be able to share God's word with the Indians.

Thomas L. carved Scripture on trees and spelled out words with rocks for the Indians to find. The more English they learned, the greater their opportunity to learn to read and write. Then they could read the Bible.

Thomas often said, "The day I saw the Indians on the Trail of Tears, my life was forever changed." I think Thomas left his mark on the trails west, but for now, I am thankful he is home. It seems that Charles now has growing pains to go west. He and his friend, Daniel Fulbright, talk about it often.

It was such a pretty day, Thomas L. and I walked to the cross in the woods. The May apples were just beginning to bloom. As we got closer, we could see someone bent down on one knee at the cross. It was Charles. We did not disturb him but instead went back to the house.

I was ashamed I had not thought about Charles's hurting heart.

Early Spring 1855

Hundreds of thousands of settlers had crossed the mountains and plains to settle in the west. The Indians were forced to give up their land to the settlers. Thomas L. Catts knew that if the white settlers or the Indians were going to survive, they had to be able to communicate. Each Indian tribe had their own language or "tongue" as they called it. The settlers had one language, English. To talk peace, they had to understand each other. To find peace, they had to understand God.

Trains were also going west. America struggled to keep up with the construction demands for tracks and bridges to carry the trains. On November 1, 1855, the Pacific Railroad's first train from St. Louis to Jefferson City steamed out of the depot while band music played.

Six-hundred prominent citizens were invited guests on the inaugural journey. The rail bridge over the Gasconade River was in question as to whether it was safe. To accommodate the railroad, trusses and braces were hurriedly built under the bridge for support

That Thursday morning, the massive train rolled onto the bridge, the trestle shuddered and then collapsed. The locomotive and many train cars plunged into the muddy river. Sadly, thirty people died and seventy-five were injured. An investigation was done that concluded the bridge had not been safe. This tragedy caused the railroad companies to proceed with caution. However, they kept building, and trains steamed their way west.

April 1856

Election Day was a celebration day for our family. This year George was elected to serve as Treasurer for Lawrence County. The people in Mount Vernon had seen his honest and trustworthy way of running the Mount Vernon Mercantile, so they elected him to take care of the county's money.

Now that Mary Ann is doing some better and their children are older, they will be able to help George at the mercantile while he does his job for the county.

Thomas L. is proud for his brother, and he carved him a wooden desk sign that reads, "George Neal Catts, County Treasurer, Lawrence County Missouri.

Not wanting to miss the excitement, Robert, Jane Ann, and their family came to the farm for George's celebration supper. Thomas L. played his fiddle and Charles his harmonica. We did something we have not done in a long time. We laughed, and we danced together.

April 1856

Nothing ever took away the pain from losing little Clarence, but life did go on for the Catts/Crawford family. Frances talked with Mary Ann about her son, John Neal, who died from yellow fever when he was nine. She told her about her struggle with depression after his death.

Mary Ann asked her mother-in-law, Frances, "How did you get past the loss?"

Frances explained she had never gotten past her loss, but with God she was able to go through life one day at a time. While at the farm on a beautiful spring day that year, Frances took Mary Ann for a walk in the woods. Here, at the cross in the woods, Mary Ann found what she needed—peace.

Early Spring 1857

The call to "go west young man" has bitten Charles like a terrapin that will not let go until it thunders. The more I talked against Charles and Daniel Fulbright going, the more determined they are to go. They have talked about going for the last three years. And they have worked to earn the money to buy one-thousand head of cattle.

What do either of them know about a cattle drive west? Thomas L. told them the unimaginable problems they will encounter. He once watched a lightning strike in the prairie kill more than a hundred cows. Also, he heard about when ornery cowpokes who came back from town liquored up and trying to shoot the stars out of the sky. It caused a stampede, and over three-hundred cows that couldn't see in the dark ran off a cliff into the river.

Thomas L. took Charles by the palm of his hand. He gave him a silver compass. The one my brother, John Neal, had given him for his sixth birthday. He told him he was only letting him borrow it and to be sure he gave it back. I think that was Thomas's way of telling Charles he wanted to be sure he would come home.

I wake up at night wondering what his father, Thomas Crawford, would tell Charles. He is headstrong and determined. I will try to stay quiet, and maybe he will change his mind. My place is on my knees.

Early Spring 1857

Unlike the other Catts/Crawford boys, Charles was bullheaded and strong willed. Once he made up his mind, not anything nor anyone was going to change it. But whatever he decided to do, he did it with all his might.

> *April 15, 1857*
>
> *Robert advised Charles to write his will before setting out for California. For me to think about him writing a will makes me consider that he might never come home. I will not let myself be that weak in my faith. He is in God's hands, not mine. Maybe I held on too tightly to him after his father died, but now it is his time to be free.*
>
> *The day has come for Charles to depart. The food is cooked, and I sit waiting on the porch for my family to arrive for our going away supper for him. His saddle bags are packed, and he is raring to go. He and Daniel will ride to Sedalia in the morning. The cattle are waiting to walk two-thousand miles west to California. I am the first to say that I don't understand the cattle business, but two-thousand miles is a long way to walk, only to be used for someone's supper when they get there. Charles will find the Bible and the goodbye letter I have written him.*
>
> *I hear a wagon coming up the road. Before I stop writing, I will make myself a promise. I will not let Charles see me cry.*
>
> *I will hold my tears until tomorrow.*

April 15, 1857

The stockyards in Sedalia, Missouri, could be smelled ten miles away. To Charles and Daniel, they were the smell of money and adventure. They had a head filled with confidence and the foolishness of a dream calling them west. The Crawford/Fulbright cattle drive pulled out of Sedalia on April 17, 1857.

June 1858

I had never met my oldest granddaughter, Fannie. She stayed behind in Virginia to finish her schooling at the Girls Academy when George and Mary Ann moved to Missouri. She came to Missouri after she graduated and has been spending time with me. Since Charles is gone, I am so glad she was there when I got the letter from Daniel Fulbright. It came by Butterfield Stage and Thomas L. brought it home to me.

Dear Mrs. Crawford,

It is with my deepest sorrow that I have to tell you that Charles died on May twenty-first. A yoke of our oxen had been stolen from a corral. Charles and two other men were tracking those that stole the ox. They got into a skirmish, and Charles was hit in his upper leg with an Indian arrow. The two men carried him in a sling a long distance and over a mountain.

When they stopped, Charles was in tremendous pain. He begged them to pull the arrow out instead of pushing it through as it should have been. The arrowhead broke off in his leg and infection set in. He died three days later at Honey Lake in the Utah Territory. We buried Charles under a tree and carved his name on a cross as a grave marker. May he rest there in peace.

You would have been proud of him, Mrs. Crawford. While he was dying, he asked the men to get his Bible from his saddle bag. Charles said it is the one you gave him. He asked that Scripture be read over him until he died. And in his last moments, he said you taught him many Scriptures when he was a young boy

In a whispering, weak voice, he said "The Lord is my shepherd, I shall not want ..." When he finished saying the Psalm, he peacefully closed his eyes.

Charles was the best friend I will ever have, and I will always miss him.

In the suitcase are the things he wanted me to send home to you. Charles told one of the men that he wanted to be sure the silver compass Thomas let him borrow was returned to him.

Charles loved you and all of his family very much.

With a saddened heart of grief,

Daniel Fulbright.

July 1858

I have walked to the cross in the woods every day since I got Daniel's letter. It has been my hiding place where no one except God can see me cry. I will not ask God why.

Thomas L. has been hurt deeply by his brother's death. Some days I think more than me. He finds an excuse why he cannot walk with me to the cross. He will go when his heart is ready. He was fourteen when Charles was born. No brother could have loved a younger brother more than Thomas L. did. He has carved a sign with Charles's name on it for the family cemetery. Since Charles will not have a gravestone, he feels it is the least he can do so his brother will not be forgotten.

"I will lift up mine eyes unto the hills, from whence cometh my help. My help cometh from the Lord which made heaven and earth" *(Psalm 121:1-2).*

Help me, Lord, to have a thankful heart.

July 1858

Frances and Thomas L. both struggled through the days after they received Daniel Fulbright's letter. Charles was only twenty-seven years old when he died. In his will, he left everything to his mother, Frances.

July 1859

It has been over a year since I found out Charles died. Daniel Fulbright returned safely home with his wife and child. They come out to visit me often. When I am sad, I walk slowly through the woods to a place I can rest—the cross.

Thomas L. does not know that I know that he goes to the cross often. I am glad he is no longer mad at God.

I saw a wild turkey meandering at the woods edge. I thought about the big turkey Charles shot one Thanksgiving. I laughed then about how he bragged on himself and I still do.

Robert is doing well in his business and has purchased more land in town and outside of town. He thinks if we don't go to war, the land will be quiet valuable. His father, Thomas Crawford, told him if he has land, he is blessed with a place to live and a place to grow your own food.

George and his family call Missouri their home. It took a while, but as long as he keeps having his special five-cent sales, he will have customers. He told me he has secretly ordered a piano for Mary Ann's Christmas gift. Not for this Christmas or the next. The piano builder has so many orders for his custom pianos that it will take a long time to build and have it delivered to Missouri. He has asked that a heart like one he carved on a cherry wood box he made for her many years ago, be carved on the piano. It too will say, "To my sweet Mary Ann," above the keys. As everyone says, they are a true love story.

Fannie is still staying with me. She enjoys keeping me company. She likes to read to me as practice for when she reads to her students. I do love having her close.

July 1859

War is all that is talked about in town and anywhere people gather to learn of the latest news.

CHAPTER 12

November 6, 1860

Abraham Lincoln was elected President of the United States of America today. With all the talk of war and secession, I hope he will lead us as "the united states." All people talk about is war. Some are saying we have no choice but to go to war. Poor Mr. Lincoln has big decisions to make.

I would like to push away the world and keep what family I have left to myself. Those that are pushing for the war have no idea the price all Americans will pay. I have been through wars, and I do know the heartache of that price.

I pray God will be with us, protect us, and give President Abraham Lincoln the wisdom to guide us away from war.

1860

South Carolina was the first state to secede from the Union on December 20, 1860. A civil war was coming, and there would be no turning back.

April 1861

Whispers about war echo all around. Every trip to town the whispers get louder, "War is coming, war is imminent." Memories rush through my mind from the past. I can almost hear the frightening sounds from rockets exploding and smell the stench from destructive burning fires. My heart sinks low as I petition God to not let war come again.

I am happy for Fannie. The young man she has promised her love to is a fine young man. Jane Ann has almost finished her beautiful wedding dress with glass buttons and has made her a white lace purse to match. With all that is happening, I hope Fannie will be still enough long enough for her to fit the dress. I am thankful Fannie has stayed with me since Charles died. Since not knowing her until she was almost eighteen, I do love my time with her.

April 12, 1861 Fort Sumter, South Carolina

An early morning ocean breeze gently lifted the United States flag flying over Fort Sumter. Thirty-three gleaming white stars on a blue background with each representing a proud state of our Union. Thirteen bold red and white strips waved with elegant grace as a reminder of our original thirteen colonies. However, by the day's end, we would be united no more.

Overwhelming disagreements over slavery, trade, and the rights of each state exploded. The southern states organized soldiers of the Confederacy to fire upon Union troops at Fort Sumter near Charleston, South Carolina. The attack was swift and quick. The Confederate soldiers had control of the fort in less than twenty-four hours.

The undeclared war of the rebellion against the United States of America had begun. It took weeks for the news to spread across the country that the Civil War had started at Fort Sumter. Sadly, no one could have imagined the cruel and destructive days ahead that would so deeply divide the country. And certainly, no one could comprehend the lives that would be lost in the dark days to come.

> *July 12, 1861*
>
> *I refuse for my heart to be torn by the war. I see the destructive question of who is right and who is wrong deeply dividing families with hate. Brother against brother and father against son, hate is the enemy to their soul. But I refuse to let what I cannot control divide my heart against my sons. I have my own feeling about the war, but from this day forward, I will not take sides for the sake of my family. My silence will be my loudest voice to those I love.*

July 12, 1861

The Catts/Crawford family stood together in their strong support for the Union. Robert was elected in 1861 to the Constitutional Convention from the Eighteenth Senatorial

District for Lawrence County, Missouri. At the Convention in Jefferson City, he voted for Missouri to remain in the Union. Missouri was the only state that officially voted to remain in the Union, but the underlying divided feelings remained.

However, on May tenth, an incident occurred near Saint Louis that became known as the Camp Jackson Affair. Union soldiers led by General Nathaniel Lyon captured some neutral state militia soldiers at Camp Jackson. The militia had planned to attack the federal arsenal in Saint Louis to obtain their munitions. Instead, Lyon captured the militia soldiers and marched them through town. An accidental gunshot created anger, fear, and instant chaos in the people. Lyon's soldiers fired into the crowd. Twenty-eight people were killed, and dozens were injured. Violence continued and ended only when martial law was imposed.

Robert heard about the Camp Jackson Affair, and as an attorney who knew the law, he felt as if the Union had attacked their own people in a state that voted to remain in the Union. From this point forward, Robert pledged his allegiance to the Pro-Confederate Missouri State Guard. Not because he was for slavery, but from a legal aspect, he was for state's rights.

Robert left home to join with the militia in the Battle of Carthage, or as some called it, the Battle of Dry Fork. It was a celebrated victory for the Missouri State Guard.

On July 12, 1861, he was elected as Lieutenant Colonel Robert W. Crawford for the thirteenth Missouri Cavalry Division, Fifth Missouri Infantry, and Eighth Division of the Missouri State Guard. He was given a soldier's uniform with brass buttons. Perhaps he was elected because he attended West Point Military Academy for two years. He was presented a Soldier's Bible. And he wrote a note, giving instructions to contact

Jane Ann Catts, should he be killed. He folded the note and put the paper in his wallet with the initials R.W. C.

George Catts believed no man should own another and that we were all equal at the foot of the cross.

Thomas L. refused to go to war. He believed in following God's Ten Commandments, including, "Thou shalt not kill." Only when forced, did Thomas L. ever use a gun against another man. He watched over Robert's family while Robert was away at war and George's family later. He remained on the farm to help Frances.

The Catts/Crawford family accepted and respected one another with unconditional love.

August 9, 1861

While I picked tomatoes early this morning before the heat of the day, I suddenly felt sick all over. I don't know where Robert is or if he is alive. Thomas L. has seen Union soldiers watching the farm. If Robert comes home, they hope to capture him. For their safety, Jane Ann only tells the children Papa is away at war. She knows they are being watched also. Many area farms have been burned to the ground by Bushwhackers. When I am in town, I make it clear to everyone that I am neutral and will not support either side.

Thomas L. thinks this is perhaps why they have not attacked the farm. George has talked about joining the Union Army but knows he could face his brother in battle. I think it is his love for Mary Ann and his family that keeps him from joining. But if a battle is near, he will go. We have been at war for just a few months, and, sadly, the heartache has only just begun.

I often shamefully think that my heart has hurt enough. John, Thomas, John Neal, little Clarence, and Charles are all gone. Then I capture my thoughts and remind myself that I got to love each one of them, if only for a while. I need a walk in the woods to the place I find peace.

August 9, 1861

Twenty-three miles east from Mount Vernon, over twelve-thousand Missouri State Guard soldiers camped in the corn fields above Wilson's Creek down on the Wire Road. Their victory at Carthage the month before opened a floodgate of new recruits for the Guard and gave them confidence and more soldiers for their next battle. They planned to attack the Union soldiers camped in Springfield, where Union General Lyon had marched more soldiers in from Rolla.

Lyon received word that the Guard was camped on the creek. He readied more than five-thousand soldiers for an all-night march for a surprise attack on the Missouri Guard.

The battle would begin at sunrise.

August 10, 1861

I could feel the war getting closer like a distant storm that makes your bones ache down deep. I was up at sunrise helping Thomas L. and Fannie feed the animals when I saw a dust cloud stirring up down the road.

As he neared, the young rider on horseback yelled, "Soldiers are fighting at Wilson Creek down by the Wire Road! The cornfields are full of Confederate soldiers, and Union soldiers have marched in from Springfield!" He turned and rode away.

I felt like a giant bolder fell from the sky, crushing my heart. I looked at Thomas L. and Fannie, and without saying a word, I turned and walked away. I went into the house and fell to my knees on the old rag-rug beside my bed. Shaking and barely able to utter the words, I began.

"Our Father, who art in heaven, hallowed by thy name; thy kingdom come, thy will be done ..."

I kept saying "Thy will be done" over and over again. That was the only prayer I could ask God to answer. I knew my sons would face each other on the battlefield today.

Fannie helped Thomas L. finish feeding the animals, and then she went over to sit on the porch. I heard someone ride up on a horse. I looked out the window and saw her fiancé. They talked for a while, and then I heard him get on his horse and ride away.

155

FAITH IS NOT SILENT

Fannie yelled out to him, "I will love you until the day I die!" I knew he must be headed off to Wilson Creek.
Hours have gone by and we still have no word.

August 10, 1861

Robert had been camped with his soldiers in a corn field. He got word that the Union troops were five miles away. Needing to be alone with God, he walked down by Wilson Creek to water his horse before the battle. He got down on his knees to pray and took his Soldier's Bible from his shirt pocket to read. Then he looked up at the white puffy clouds above and prayed out loud. "Our Father who art in heaven, hallowed be thy name. Thy kingdom come, thy will be done."

Hearing someone behind him, he turned and saw two little girls, each carrying a bucket. He stood, put his Bible back in his shirt pocket, and reached for the buckets. He filled them with water and told them, "Run home and tell your papa there are soldiers in the corn field." Robert went back to his men and waited for the Union soldier to arrive.

The young rider rode from the farm into town, yelling, "The soldiers are fighting at Wilson Creek down by the Wire Road— thousands of 'em!"

People came out when they heard the commotion. Some loaded their guns and prepared to fight.

George was sweeping the porch at the mercantile when he heard. He grabbed the money from the cash drawer, his gun, and all the ammunition he had on the shelf. He locked the door and then went to the court house to get the cash box containing the county's money. To protect the county money, he buried the cash box and went to his family to give them the cash from the mercantile.

Already knowing in her heart that George would go to the battle, Mary Ann met him at the door with his saddle bag packed with food and water. They hugged and held each other close. The children came out and gathered around him.

William, his oldest son, squeezed his Papa's hand and began, "Our Father who art in heaven …" Together they prayed. William ran to saddle up his father's best horse while he said his goodbyes.

George held Mary Ann one last time before mounting his horse. Squeezing her hand, he said, "Set me a plate. I'll be home for supper." Mary Ann and the children watched as he rode away.

By the time George reached Wilson Creek, the battle was in full force. He grabbed his gun and cautiously ran up the hill where he heard a cannon fire and looked for blue-uniformed soldiers. Running to join them, he fell in line for battle. As soldiers fell either injured or dead all around him, he stayed as close to blue-uniformed soldiers as possible. Without a uniform on himself, he knew he was a target for both sides.

Colonel Crawford charged his cavalry men up and down the rolling hills, attacking the Union soldiers. With every booming cannon, men were thrust into the air by the flying shrapnel, dropping to the ground either dead or badly injured.

As Colonel Crawford charged up Bloody Hill, his horse was shot out from under him, throwing him to the ground. Still down, he heard men moaning in pain all around him. He looked up and saw his beloved brother, George, lying nearby. He started to stand and felt something hit his chest, knocking him backward. Trying to rise up, he felt to see if he was bleeding. Rubbing his hand over his chest, he felt the Soldier's Bible in his shirt pocket. Still lying on the ground, he removed the Bible from his pocket and held it up. A warm bullet was stuck in the Bible.

Raising up on his knees and using his sword to defend himself, he crawled over to George. He dragged him off the field and under a tree. Accessing his wounds, he discovered his left leg and shoulder were injured. He stuffed his handkerchief into George's shoulder wound and found a fallen tree limb nearby to use as a crutch to get George to his feet.

Pulling a pencil and paper from his pocket, he wrote a note that said, "Place this soldier on the next available medical wagon to Springfield. By command of Colonel Robert Crawford, August 10, 1861." He turned to George and saw a medical wagon coming up the hill. He flagged it down, showed the driver the note, and helped load George onto the wagon.

While the driver helped load other soldiers, Robert put the note in his pocket, grabbed George's hand, and prayed for him.

George squeezed his hand tightly, looked into his brother's eyes, and said, "Forever blood brothers."

Robert nodded and watched the medical wagon pull away, his brother inside.

He stepped back out onto the battlefield just as a soldier rode up with a horse for him. Colonel Robert Crawford mounted his horse and rode back into battle.

The battle at Wilson Creek raged on for more than five hours in the hot summer heat. More than twenty-three hundred soldiers were killed, wounded, or missing when the battle ended. Unknown numbers died along the roads going home.

Unbeknown to the family, and though separated by war, they all said the Lord's Prayer at exactly the same time.

September 1861

It has been over two weeks since the battle at Wilson Creek, and we have no idea if George or Robert are still alive. Poor Mary Ann has set a place at the table for George at every meal, still hoping he will come home. The white china plate keeps hope in her heart. Finally, she received a letter from George. He told her he was in the hospital in Springfield. He said his wounds are healing, and he will be home soon, and to tell everyone how much he loves them.

I am glad Robert told Jane Ann to come to Mount Vernon so she will be close to family. We agreed to keep our normal schedule for Sundays. First church, then family lunch at the farm, and sometimes they would all stay the night. That way when the Union soldiers who are on lookout for Robert see Jane Ann coming and going at the farm, they will not be suspicious. Robert had one of his men secretly deliver a note to her this morning. He asked her to meet him at the cross in the woods Sunday night.

Thomas L. told Jane Ann, "Follow the light to the cross."

Long after dark, Thomas L. went to the barn and let our old, slow mule, Poke-A-Long, get loose. He lit a lantern as a signal to Robert and headed to the woods. Acting like he was trying to find the mule, he would call her name just in case there were Union soldiers hiding in the woods watching the house.

Jane Ann slipped out the back door and followed a good distance behind the lantern. She went to the cross and waited. Soon, Robert stepped out from behind a tree. Jane Ann told me later that they knew not to talk, so they instead held each other close. Without saying a word, they passed each other a letter. Robert turned to walk away. He stopped, reached out to hug her one last time, then slipped away into the dark woods.

Thomas L., hiding nearby, signaled to her to follow the lantern back to the house. Knowing old Poke-A-Long had not gone far, he found her and led her back to the barn while Jane Ann slipped back into the house. Lighting an oil lamp low, she huddled under it to read his letter.

He first told her how much he loved her and the family and gave her instructions for what to do if he does not come home. He then told her that since the Missouri Guard moved into Springfield after the Union retreated to Rolla, he was able to go to the hospital. Both Union and Guard wounded soldiers were being treated there.

He searched the wards until he found George. Unable to talk to him, he waited until no one was around, then he squeezed his brother's hand, gave him a nod, and turned and walked away.

While the children slept in the adjoining room, Jane Ann, Mary Ann, Thomas L., and I got on our knees and thanked God for protecting George and Robert.

September 1861

The five-hour battle at Wilson Creek left the dead lying throughout the fields. The dead were left behind while the living went on to the next battle. Some coldly say that was just the ways of war. Others keep the hope in their heart alive, waiting for the ones they love to come home. Many never return.

Fannie Catts knew in her heart when she saw her fiancé ride away that she'd never see him again. For the first few weeks, she sat on the porch and waited, hoping he'd come back. He never did. After a few weeks, she folded her beautiful white-lace wedding dress with matching purse and put them in her cedar chest, her heart aching with sadness and grief.

Mary Ann held on to George's last words he spoke to her as he rode off to battle. At every meal, she sat a place for her George at the head of the table. His favorite, white, china plate sat day after day, meal after meal, waiting for him to come home. Finally, she received a letter telling her he was in the hospital and would be home soon. So, she kept setting his place at the table.

The Missouri State Guard soldiers paroled the Springfield streets. After Wilson Creek, they regrouped, and some went on to the Battle of Charleston on August nineteenth. Colonel Crawford stayed behind with his men to prepare for a different battle. Knowing Union soldiers were on the lookout for him and other leaders of the Guard, he cautiously sent a note to his wife, Jane Ann, telling her to meet him on Sunday night. He felt he couldn't leave for the next battle without seeing her. And he knew he needed to give her the dreaded instructions of what to do if he didn't return.

After the Battle of Dry Wood Creek, or as some called it, the Battle of the Mules, Colonel Crawford headed his men north. Tired and needing water for their horses, they set up camp along a spring-fed stream. After being sure his men were settled for the night, the Colonel went alone down by the stream to wash up, to shave, and to read his Bible.

With the dim light from a lantern and a small mirror, he prepared to use the razor that had once belonged to his father. He soaped his face and leaned his head to the right. Holding the mirror in one hand, he placed the blade of the razor on his neck. Suddenly, someone jumped him from behind, grabbed the blade, and pressed it deep against the Colonel's juggler vein.

Colonel Crawford thrust his elbows backward into the ribs of his assailant, and the blade fell from his hand. Spinning around, he shoved his hands around the person's neck and squeezed tight. As he leaned forward with all his strength, the moonlight revealed the face of his attacker. A young boy no older than the Colonel's youngest son. Releasing him, he helped him stand up.

Clearing his throat and with tears in his eyes, the young boy said, "I'm lost, and I can't find my way home." The Colonel told the young boy to sit down on the stump, which was the stump he had been standing on when the boy jumped the Colonel. He handed him a cup of cold water from the stream.

The boy explained he tried to join the Union Army, but they said he was too young. Then he said, "Now I'm lost, hungry, and I don't know how to get home."

Patting his back, the Colonel told him to hide over in the bushes until he could get him some food. Going back to camp, the Colonel loaded a haversack full of food to take to the boy. While the boy was eating, Robert waited to be sure the guards didn't see him.

Quietly, Robert untied the hobble from one of the horses and walked it to where the boy was hiding. He told him he would have to ride bareback and gave him the directions he needed to get home. Helping the young boy up onto the horse, the Colonel touched his shoulder, bowed his head, and said, "Please God, get him home safely."

Throwing the haversack of food over his shoulder, the boy looked at the Colonel and said, "Sir, I pray God will bless you for your kindness to me." And he rode off into the darkness.

Colonel Crawford sat down on the stump and prayed for his sons. He then used the lantern to find his father's razor. Picking it up from the dirt, he wiped it clean and closed the blade. Realizing the vulnerable position he'd put himself in with the shaving razor, he promised himself he would not shave again until after the war.

The next morning one of the soldiers noticed a horse had pulled his hobble loose and was gone. Nothing else was said. Colonel Crawford and his soldiers continued north past Jefferson City to Lexington.

Here they encountered General Lyon's soldiers at the Siege of Lexington, also called the Battle of the Hemp Bails. At the time, hemp was grown much like hay. It was baled and mainly used to make rope. During the siege, Guard soldiers soaked the hemp bails in the Missouri River. Then they used them for protection by rolling them up the hill toward the Anderson House, where the Union soldiers were holed up. The Missouri Guard's victory was credited with the idea of using rolling bails for protection.

From there, Colonel Crawford moved his men into position for the Battle of Liberty—a victory for the Missouri Guard. However, by October the scales of victory shifted to the Union. The Battle of Osceola, the Battle of Monday's Hollow, the Battle of Fredericktown, and back to the First Battle of Springfield were all Union victories.

While Colonel Crawford was close to home, he slipped away to see his family.

October 1861

I was so thankful when Mary Ann got the letter from George. At least, she knows he is alive and being cared for in the hospital. In his letter, he mentioned Doctor Joseph King. Concerned that we had not heard from him, George and Mary Ann's daughter, Alicia, wrote a letter to the doctor and to her father. She asked the doctor if she can visit her father. Finally, she received a letter yesterday from Doctor King. He told her not to come. He said, "Typhoid fever is in every hospital ward and it would not be safe."

Two days later, Doctor King had a note delivered to Mary Ann and Alicia. He told them he was so sorry, but George had died on October ninth from typhoid fever. Included in his letter was an unfinished letter from George to Mary Ann. He wanted to be sure George's body was returned to the family for burial.

I'm glad Jane Ann and I were with Mary Ann and Alicia when they received the news. It was as if we were all stabbed in the heart with a dull, double-edged sword.

Thomas L. and Fannie came in from the yard where they had been watching all the kids play, just as Mary Ann fell to the floor crying.

George was my first son, Mary Ann's husband, brother to Jane Ann and Thomas L., and father to Alicia and Fannie. That moment of pain hurt so deeply, we all felt as if our hearts would explode.

October 1861

Thomas L. went by wagon to Springfield to bring George's body home. Thinking that George would be home soon, Jane Ann had made him a new suit. Instead, it was given to a nurse at the hospital to put on George as his burial suit. Thomas L. built the casket and dug the grave for his brother. The Catts/Crawford women again dressed in black to mourn for someone they loved. Jane Ann again wore her black gloves.

George was buried in the Catts/Crawford Cemetery next to his son, Clarence.

No one knew Robert was nearby, not even Jane Ann. When Robert heard his beloved brother, George, had died, he came home. Hidden away in the woods, he watched the funeral from afar.

After the funeral, with a cool fall breeze whispering through the air and leaves falling around them, Mary Ann, Jane Ann, Thomas L., and Frances walked to the cross in the woods. Careful not to scare them, Robert slowly stepped out from behind a tree. They circled the cross and cried together. Then Robert was gone.

Mary Ann kept setting the white china plate at the head of the table as a reminder to keep telling her children about the good man they called their Papa. She kept wearing the heart locket George gave her with his picture inside. Mary Ann never remarried. She wanted only one love story in her life, and that was with George.

Just before Christmas, a wooden crate was delivered to the Catts house in town. The piano George had ordered for Mary Ann two years before had arrived. Above the keys, a heart was carved, and inside the heart in scrolled letters was written, "To my sweet Mary Ann."

Frances never got over losing George. Or anyone she loved.

When people in town heard George had died, they grieved with the Catts/Crawford family. But it didn't take long for them to question Mary Ann about what happened to the money that was in the Lawrence County cash box the day George left to go to Wilson Creek. The question about what happened to their money never went away.

Christmas 1861

Christmas will never be the same again. Robert is away at war and so many of the ones I love are gone. I want to sit by the warm fire, stare at the burning flames and be alone. But instead I will make myself get up and cook our family Christmas Eve dinner.

Christmas 1861

The piano George gave Mary Ann sat in silence.

Dr. King stayed in touch with Alicia after George died. They later fell in love and were married.

CHAPTER 13

March 6-7, 1862

I know Robert was among the men who tried in to take the Mount Vernon Court House from the Union in February. Word was going around town that General Price, under whom Robert serves, and his men entered Mount Vernon with the intention of removing the Union flag. They instead were met with Union opposition. Some said five prisoners were taken and their flag captured.

Since Mary Ann lives in town, she went to the Court House to question who was taken prisoner. A jailer who remembered her husband, George, gave her the names.

We are so thankful Robert's name was not listed.

March 6-7, 1862

Skirmishes continued outside Mount Vernon and also in Neosho. Both the Union and the Guard robbed and pillaged the houses. To prevent soldiers from getting corn whiskey, which would cause them to be impaired, Pennington's and Mallard's still-houses on Stall's Creek north of Mount Vernon were destroyed.

By order of General Price, Colonel Crawford's Thirteenth Cavalry was sent into Arkansas to the Battle of Pea Ridge, also known as the Battle of Elkhorn Tavern—a bitter two-day battle with over ten thousand Union soldiers against sixteen thousand Confederate and Guard soldiers. Casualties and losses were high—thirteen hundred for the Union and two thousand for the Confederate and Guard soldiers. The Union took the victory.

Later General Price reported, "Colonel Robert Crawford distinguished himself as on former occasions for his gallantry and true courage."

From there, General Price included Colonel Crawford's Thirteenth Cavalry in orders to prepare to move. Each man was to be given thirty rounds of ammunition. They were given one wagon for every fifteen men that would carry tents, bedding, and cooking utensils and were to be ready to move out by his command.

The Thirteenth was then sent down into Texas to recruit more soldiers. They may have doubled back for the First Battle of Newtonia before going to Texas for more recruits.

Summer 1862

Thomas Crawford always said, "What we are aware of, we are responsible for." I knew the Bushwhackers and Renegades were roaming Lawrence County, burning the farms of those sympathetic to the south. So, I decided our family should be ready if they did come our way. Since Jane Ann, Mary Ann, and all the children were at the farm with me quite often, I planned a job for everyone, and we practiced so we would be ready for whatever might happen.

I always keep warm molasses on the back of the stove in case anybody came who might want a cold biscuit with molasses. And I always keep soapy, hot water on the stove in case anybody needs a bath. I also learned that a small shelf over each doorway might provide you with just what you need, when you need it.

Summer 1862

Thomas had gone to Springfield to pick up supplies. Those who wanted to do harm must have been watching the house and must have known he was gone. Two bad-looking men rode up on their horses and tied them up out front. At first, they wanted food, so Frances put another log in the stove and waited for it to get hot.

They sat down at the table and made themselves at home. Then they started questioning where they might find Colonel Crawford and if anybody knew where George Catts hid the cash box that contained the county's money. Nervously tapping their fingers on the table, they were about to make their move.

One of them raised his voice and said, "I'm going to hurt somebody if I don't find out what I want to know!"

Frances reached over and locked the front door. The kids knew to take their places to start their plan of action.

Mary Ann and Helen grabbed a cane and pulled their chairs out from under the men.

Jane Ann reached for a big pot of soapy hot water and poured the water on them.

Fannie took the hot molasses from the stove and poured molasses on their heads and chest.

Little Thomas Neal and Ida got big hammers and pounded their knees and hands.

Frances stepped over to get a pot of turnip greens with lots of extra lard. She poured the hot greasy greens all over those mean men. They rolled and kicked and hollered as they tried to get up off the floor.

Sweet little Cora Bell did her job too. She opened the back door.

Helen reached up to get a bag of corn chops and chicken feed from above the door. Just as the men slid out of the back door, she threw the feed all over them. Every chicken and duck in the yard jumped on them. They pecked their head and backs. Trying to knock the chickens off, they stood up to run. As they were not able to see where they were going, Lucy opened the gate to the pig pen.

They slipped and slid in everything the pigs had left behind. Meanwhile, the pigs tried to bite the corn chops stuck in the molasses. Thomas Neal then opened the far side of the pig pen so they could run that direction, which led straight out to where the old outhouse had been. People didn't build a new outhouse back then. They dug a new hole and moved the outhouse. Then they filled the old hole with lime and dirt. Thomas L. had dug a new hole and moved the outhouse closer to the barn. He had put some boards over the old hole until he had time to fill it with lime and dirt.

When the two bushwhackers ran out of the pig pen, Thomas Neal shut the gate so the pigs wouldn't follow them.

William and Fannie were waiting for the men and immediately pulled the boards away from the outhouse hole and ran to the house. There they could watch from the back porch with everyone else. Running and screaming wildly, the two men suddenly disappeared from sight.

A rope had been tied to a nearby tree in case it was ever needed. The family watched as the men used the rope to climb out of the hole. William had already brought their horses around to the back of the house. When the men started running, Frances slapped the horse's rumps, and they took off at a gallop.

The men tried to jump on their horses when they ran by, but they were so greasy they slid off. Still hollering, they ran off south of the farm, and Frances didn't think they were ever seen in Lawrence County again.

February 1863

Everyone knows that the tiny seeds of lettuce and spinach must be planted by Valentine's Day if you want tender, not bitter, leaves. Thomas L. had already plowed our garden for me to plant. Thinking about Mary Ann, he said he was going into town to prepare her garden. It was an unusually warm February day and a difficult day for us all.

Robert had been in many battles, along with his two sons, Joel and John T.M., and Daniel Fulbright, the one Charles took the cattle to California with, had served under his command. The Missouri Guard was running short of supplies and men. He had been asked by General Price to take wagons and horses down to Texas to recruit new soldiers. Knowing he would be gone for an extended time, he took Jane Ann and the family with him.

I miss her every day. Fannie went into town to stay with her mother after George died. The first of February was Mary Ann and little Clarence's birthday. Today would have been George's fiftieth birthday, and tomorrow Charles would have been thirty-two. I wanted to stay home, and Mary Ann had earlier said she too wanted to stay home. We both just wanted to wish the day away.

Instead, I planted my lettuce and then sat quietly pondering my memories.

February 1863

Eighteen months had passed since George died, nine years since little Clarence had died, and soon to be five years since Charles was killed in California. The day was not a good one for Frances or Mary Ann.

Thomas L. had tried to cheer up Mary Ann, but her sorrow was too deep, and George's death still hurt like an open wound. She assured Thomas L. she would plant the seeds. Putting on a coat, she went out with her hand spade to dig a shallow trench. Bending down to start digging, without warning, anger filled her heart. Digging deeper and deeper with the spade, she got madder and madder until she finally was jabbing the spade into the dirt. Suddenly, she realized she was hitting something metal. Digging around it and under the edge, Mary Ann lifted out a metal cash box. She'd been digging where George had planted a rose garden for her. She always planted her lettuce at the edge before the roses came up in the spring.

She took the metal box into the house and hid it in a cabinet.

After the children were in bed and the house was quiet, Mary Ann took the dirty metal box and set it on the table. Dirt was still pressed into the corners and on top of the box that had been buried for almost two years. She sat staring at it in the dimly lit room with only one oil lamp in the corner to give her light and thought about the many people who had questioned what

George did with the county's money. All the rude remarks about her keeping the money ran through her mind.

Still staring at the box, she realized there was no lock on the cash box. George must have been in such a hurry, he forgot to lock it. Thinking back, she remembered he'd been doing something in the garden before he came into the house to tell her he was going to Wilson Creek. To protect the money, he buried the cash box, and to protect his family, he didn't tell anyone where he hid the money.

She reached over and opened the box. Just as she thought, it was filled with money.

Mary Ann sat in almost darkness with the low light from the oil lamp flickering as if it were burning out of oil. Had God left the money in the rose garden for her to find? With seven children to raise on her own, only he would know how much she needed the money. Then she thought about George and how honored he was that people in the county trusted him with their money. Oddly, the light in the corner started to shine brighter and brighter.

Mary Ann slowly reached for the box and closed it. Standing up, she picked it up and put it in a basket. Laying a table cloth over the top, she set the basket on the table.

The next morning, Valentine's Day, she told her children about their father being treasurer of Lawrence County and how the people trusted him with their money. They all got dressed, put on their coats, and walked over to the court house. With her children standing beside her, she asked if she could make a deposit to the county in the name of George Catts, former Treasurer of Lawrence County. She cleared his name. Like everyone said, "George and Mary Ann were forever a love story."

And the piano George had given Mary Ann for Christmas ... she finally was able to play.

Spring 1864

Mary Ann received a telegram letting her know that her son, John Campbell Catts, was being sent home from the Academy in Virginia. He had been ill for some time, and the school thought it best to send him home.

The train line goes only as far as Rolla Missouri. Thomas L. was asked to take the wagon and pick up John Campbell at the train station, let him rest, and if he is able to lie in the bed of the wagon, to bring him home.

I will sit on the porch and pray for Thomas L. as he travels to Rolla. He will take almost two weeks to get there.

Spring 1864

John Campbell was pale and weak when Thomas picked him up. He refused to rest but instead wanted to hurry home. Perhaps he knew he was dying and wanted to see his Mama one last time.

Thomas L. made him as comfortable as he could for the one-hundred-and-fifty-mile trip home. But the long, bumpy road toward Mount Vernon was hard on John Campbell. With every bump, he moaned in pain. And then the moaning stopped. Pulling the wagon over to check on him, Thomas found he had died.

Rain began to pour down and the skies were darkening. Thomas L. had to make a decision. He knew the creeks and roads would be flooded and had no idea how long getting home would take him. He decided to bury John Campbell on a hilltop under a big oak tree. Just as he had done with Sara Ann, he carved his name on the tree and made a cross with his name. And in between the rain, he went down by the river and dug flowers to plant on his grave.

How could he tell Mary Ann or Frances that John Campbell had died? Both had husbands, small children, and now sons who died and were buried far away. Fairness had nothing to do with anyone's life.

Fall 1864

God created the heart of man for good, not for hate and destruction. I don't understand how a heart can hate whom they don't know or why they can choose to destroy what is not theirs. And I will never understand how they can ride away into the darkness and never look back at the lives they destroyed.

My first response to my enemy will be my heart's response. So, I must ask myself, what is in the deepest part of who I am? Rather than argue with God and try to explain away why I have the right to hate my enemy, I will humble my heart and do it His way.

Fall 1864

On the last day of October, the Catts/Crawford farm was ready for winter. The Farmer's Almanac predicted a cold winter, as did the persimmons, wooly-worms, and the thick fur on the animals. The root-cellar had bushel baskets overflowing with potatoes, turnips, sweet potatoes, and apples lined up and ready to use. Mason canning jars lined the shelves and showed off the summer vegetable colors needed to make soups and stews. Jellies, jams, and apple-butter awaited buttermilk biscuits. The barn was filled with hay. Slow-smoked hams and bacon hung in the smokehouse, and barrels with pecans and walnuts waited to be cracked for Christmas candy.

And the family was all hoping Jane Ann and Robert would be able to come home.

Fannie stayed at the farm to help finish the winter readiness and to pack. Sadly, the packing was with the expectation of Bushwhackers attacking the farm. Three farms had been attacked the past week and the Catts/Crawford farm was probably next on their road to flaming destruction.

They had done all they could do to be prepared for what they expected to come to them any day.

In darkness. the Bushwhackers came with evil in their hearts and flaming torches in their hands.

Frances, Thomas L., and Fannie were awakened by loud voices. Thomas peeked out and saw six men on horses, their faces covered, flaming torches held high.

Prepared as Frances always was, her most treasured possessions were boxed and stacked by the back door. She reached for the wooden sign hanging on the mantel and her flag box.

Fannie got the family Bible and Frances's journal from beside her bed.

Thomas reached for his shotgun. He was ready to use a gun only if they forced his hand. He ran out the back door to the back side of the barn to let the animals go free. Fannie and Frances carried the boxes out back as far as they could get them from the house. Grabbing armloads of quilts, dragging out chairs and a table, they ran back inside one more time.

The first three flaming torches were thrown into the barn and another into the hen coup. The next three were thrown into the house. Then two were thrown onto the roof, obviously to assure complete destruction.

Thomas had buckets filled with water and feed sacks to beat out the flames, but they did no good. Everything was gone. The cold-hearted ones accomplished their goal and burned everything to the ground.

"But I say unto you, love your enemies, bless them that curse you, do good to them that hate you, and pray for them which despitefully use you and persecute you" (Matthew 5:44, KJV).

The Catts/Crawford family was thankful for the items that were saved and for the food stored in the root-cellar. The sickening smoldering smell reminded Frances of when the British burned Washington, D.C. Standing in sad silence, Frances raised her hand and began to sing, "Amazing Grace, how sweet the sound that saved a retch like me ..."

Neighbors and friends came the next morning to help them build a one-room cabin for winter and a shed for the animals.

April 1865
Will it ever end? We have lost most everything. Will it ever be well with my soul again? I think about America and ask the same questions, "Will it ever end?" And if it does, will it ever be well with the soul of our nation again? Weary from war and with the deepest wounds, can we ever forgive one another and be united again? Only with God can our broken hearts be healed and have the strength to forgive. May the words of my beloved friend echo in my heart and the heart of our nation, "In God is our trust."

April 1865

After hundreds of thousands of husbands, fathers, and sons died, and we destroyed our own nation, one man stepped forward to surrender to another.

The tipping point of the Civil War was when General Robert E. Lee surrendered to General Ulysses S. Grant at the Appomattox Court House in Virginia on April 9, 1864.

That news was followed five days later with headlines, "President Abraham Lincoln Assassinated." While attending a performance at Ford's Theater, in Washington, DC, on April 14, 1865, he was fatally shot by John Wilkes Booth. President Lincoln died the following morning.

Many people later said Lincoln was the last man killed in the Civil War. So weary from the long war, perhaps President Lincoln prayed, "Whatever it takes to end this war, Lord, thy will be done." Some thought he meant even if it meant giving his own life.

Some said President Lincoln's death was the final blow to our nation's heart that caused soldiers to throw down their guns and walk away. Draped in black, our nation grieved for our president and grieved even more for what the people had done to one another.

But war was finally over.

Jane Ann Crawford had returned to Missouri with family in 1864.

The war now over, Robert returned, broke financially and broken in health. He had lost almost everything. Not having shaved during the war, his children didn't recognize him when he returned. He used his father's razor to shave so his children could see he was the same man who loved them before the war and the same man who loved them even more after the war.

When he went to see his mother, he found her and Thomas L. waiting at the end of the road to welcome him home. Mary Ann, never bitter that her husband George died after Wilson Creek, welcomed Robert home. The partially written letter that Doctor King returned to Mary Ann after George died told the story of how Robert helped him on the battlefield as a blood brother, not as an enemy.

George and Mary Ann's son, William, had joined the Union as a drummer boy after his father died in 1861. He told them he was seventeen but was really only twelve. He returned after the war and later played with John Phillip Sousa before Sousa became well known. And he was a charter member in the Mount Vernon Brass Band.

America moved forward, one restored heart at a time.

If my people which are called by my name, shall humble themselves, and pray, and seek my face, and turn from their wicked ways; then will I hear from heaven, and will forgive their sin, and will heal their land (II Chronicles 7:14).

CHAPTER 14

1866

I am thankful every day that the war is over. And that I can gratefully say again, "I thank you Heavenly Father for another good day that has come and gone, let your healing continue."

1866

America was rebuilding what had been destroyed during the war, including the heart and soul of our nation.

Thomas L. Crawford, his neighbors, and friends built a new house and barn on the Catts/Crawford farm. Then they helped someone else, and then someone else.

1869

Life seems somewhat normal for a change. Robert has become a prominent lawyer in the surrounding counties and has earned the respect of those he works with. Jane Ann is the forever caregiver in the family, never taking sides and only caring and loving everyone. Thomas not only runs the farm but also takes care of Mary Ann and the family's needs. She has been widowed for over eight years and said she will never marry again.

I thought I would never remarry after John died, but after so many years alone, I fell in love with Thomas Crawford. I have always wondered if Thomas L. ever fell in love while on the Oregon Trail. He once mentioned a lady's name. I think it was Sara Ann. But he seems content to be a farmer and woodworker. Fannie is happy. She never married but knows with all her heart she is doing what God planned for her to do with her life.

Now close to eighty, I am very content to be with my family.

1869

Robert worked hard serving as a lawyer in several counties. However, he and others felt they must accomplish something before they'd be at peace after the war. Hundreds of Missouri State Guard and Confederate soldiers were killed at Wilson

Creek and over three hundred at the battle for Springfield. But they had no place to be buried. Most bodies had been left on the fields or buried in shallow graves.

The National Cemetery in Springfield was established in 1867 as a place of honor for Civil War soldiers. And generations to come would have a resting place for those who died serving our country.

The Confederate Association was established, and four acres of land adjoining the National Cemetery was purchased for a Confederate Cemetery. Robert Crawford served on the board and completed all the legal filings required to set up the cemetery—the only Confederate cemetery in Missouri.

Robert, along with other members, went to Wilson Creek to find the remains of the fallen Confederate soldiers. They dug up the remains and brought them back to Springfield for burial.

They searched the area where the battle for Springfield occurred and dug any remains that were found and buried them also.

There are over five hundred graves in the Confederate Cemetery, but only four have names on the gravestones.

The first Decoration Day for the Confederate Cemetery occurred on June 1870, five years after the war ended.

October 1873

I carried my burdens and pain to the cross in the woods many times after the war. Gradually, my load became lighter each time I willingly let go.

I was thankful to see Robert and Jane Ann so happy. Then Robert suddenly died. My heart hurt for Jane Ann when I thought about all they had gone through during the war. I may not have always agreed with Robert, but I respected his devotion to stand strong for what he believed to be right. He followed his heart to do the right thing even when he put himself in danger. He was never a perfect man, but he was an honorable man.

From the day I married his father, Thomas Crawford, he became my son, and I became his mother. I will grieve for him just as deeply as I did for George, Charles, and John Neal. And I will pour my tears upon the cross with a grateful heart that he was my son.

October 1873

After losing everything they owned during the war, Robert and Jane Ann returned to Mount Vernon to rebuild their lives. Due to his strong stance for state's rights and his support for the Confederacy, his family paid a heavy price. His support was not for slavery but for the legal rights of each state. However, he was labeled as a southern sympathizer in a state that was split in their support.

When his mother's farm was burned by Bushwhackers, he assumed he was to blame. No one in the family ever blamed Robert, only those who chose to take the law into their own hands. So, with his family's support and encouragement, he was able to rebuild a successful law practice. He was a prominent lawyer, respected by all who worked with him. Perhaps Robert's golden rule helped him succeed as a lawyer before and after the war.

He said, "Never look down on anyone, only God sits that high."

While attending court in Nevada, Missouri, Robert collapsed in the courtroom from pneumonia. Jane Ann came to be at his side. He told her he always wondered if the young boy who tried to kill him ever made it home to his family. He said he had no regrets in his support for the Confederacy, but he regretted the problems his stance had caused his family.

He died peacefully on October 19, 1873, at age sixty-one, with Jane Ann holding his hand and telling him she loved him.

Thomas L. helped her with the arrangement and built yet another coffin for someone he loved. And Jane Ann once again laid out her black gloves and hat. People from surrounding counties came to pay their respects to the family. Robert was buried near his brother, George Catts, at the Catts/Crawford Cemetery.

For two brothers who chose opposite sides during the war to be buried in the same family cemetery was unusual. Their mother, Frances, who never took sides against either of her sons, had insisted they be buried near one another as brothers.

The Greenfield Bar Association made the following resolution after the death of Colonel Robert Crawford: "We have lost one of our brightest ornaments, society has lost a most gentle companion, an able and high-toned gentleman … a most useful and honored citizen … we must appear well at the Bar of that Supreme Tribunal before which we are all soon to submit our pleading and records …"

The Barton County Barr made the following resolutions:

"Whereas, it has pleased God in the wise dispensation of His Providence to call one of his creatures, and one of our most esteemed and beloved brethren from the labors and toils of life in the courts of this world to that Court in Heaven wherein God alone is Judge, and where the wicked cease from troubling and the weary are at rest …"

"That in taking leave of our distinguished brother, we humbly bow to the will of the Great Jehovah, who doeth all things well; before whom we too will soon be called to appear; who it is that alone giveth and taketh away. Blessed in the name of the Lord …"

"That in the life and character of our deceased brother we have an example of professional honor and ability and personal worth worthy of emulation. In him was found the warmest emotions of the husband and father, a gentleman and a strong friend …"

"That we tender our warmest sympathies to the bereaved family who has had one of its members plucked from the home circle by the rude hand of death. But in this dispensation of providence we would remind them that the one who is gone had lived beyond the usual years allotted to man, and who in the fullness of time, fell like ripe grain before the sickle of the reaper ..."

"Robert W. Crawford, may he rest in peace."

June 1876

Thomas L. and Fannie escorted me back east to America's Centennial Celebration. It took us several days to travel by train to Wellsburg. I was so excited to walk in Thomas's apple orchards once again. I knocked on the door of the house we had lived in, and we were invited to have lemonade on the porch. The new owners were so kind and said we could walk all around the farm.

Thomas L. remembered the day Thomas Crawford and I were married in the gardens behind the house when the beautiful bluish-purple hydrangeas were in bloom. He also remembered the day we left to go to Missouri, Thomas gave him the apple seed box.

He and Fannie helped me climb the fence to walk through the green field to the house where Alexander Campbell lived and where Thomas L. studied. We went to the cemetery to lay flowers on his grave and on the grave of Helen Crawford, mother of my Crawford sons. We then went to Fannie's school to see where she attended classes.

We traveled by train to Washington DC. I so loved seeing the beautiful Capitol and White House. And I was so thankful to see Frankie and Ms. Polly's house again.

As we traveled on to Baltimore, I thought about the many memories of the city where I was born. Thomas L. and I shared a special time when we went to visit his father's grave and the grave of his brother, my beloved son, John Neal. He remembered the day we danced in the rain in our new rubber galoshes. I so wish I could have seen my brother, John Neal, and my sister, Rachael, one more time before they passed away.

But I did get to see the old hat shop and the adjoining house where we lived. And I even heard the bells ring at the Old Otterbein

Church. I so loved seeing that the old fort was still standing and treasured my time just sitting in the sunshine with my memories.

Then we went on to Philadelphia to enjoy the Centennial Celebration. We had a long walk to find Robert's nephew's wooden piece of art he'd created from seventy-six different species of wood from West Virginia. His nephew's name is George B. Crawford, who named the piece Centennial Bracket, an outstanding piece that contained images celebrating our nation's heritage. And more than anything, I was surprised to see the Star-Spangled Banner flag again. And so very thankful I remembered to bring my piece of the flag with me.

As I respectfully approached the huge flag, I took out my folded treasure and laid it up to the jagged edge of the flag. Memories swirled in my mind of Christmas morning in 1814 when I gave John the piece of the flag. And how many times, when he was in pain, he would hold it. And I think about the times he told our children to hold dearly to the meaning of the flag.

He once wrote to his brother, "As long as the flag was still waving above Fort McHenry, we kept fighting. The flag was our symbol of our future, and it kept us going. It kept us united as one in the battle for our freedom. The flag was the image of our children's future, and they are why we were willing to die for the flag."

And I am so thankful to see the flag still preserved for future generations.

June 1876

Ten million people attended the Centennial Celebration in Philadelphia in 1876. The excitement filled the City of Brotherly Love. The people saw new inventions, ate new foods, and met interesting people from around the world.

And Frances was there with her piece from the most important flag in American history, folded neatly in her purse.

August 1, 1876

Fannie, who has devoted her life to serving others and teaching school, is so pleased to have been asked to serve as a collector of funds to build the new Christian Church in town. They have estimated the costs and the amount they will need to collect to begin construction. She will do a fine job in serving the church in this manner. If someone has committed to donate twenty-five dollars, she will see to it they fulfill their commitment.

I am concerned about Jane Ann. She stays to herself much too often, and her spark of joy has not returned since Robert died. She seems lost without him. I will ask her to come to the farm to help me can tomatoes and green beans. Perhaps time together will allow her to talk through her grief.

August 1, 1876

Fannie now has taught school for many years. Her students love her, and she is always coming up with something new and exciting to challenge her students. Every new book she gets, she shares with her students. Parents express how thankful they are for Fannie Catts.

Summer 1878

I attended the dedication service at the Christian Church with Fannie. She was so proud to see the church completed and that the money she collected to build the church was used wisely.

Thomas L. has promised he will take me to Springfield where I can see a new invention called the telephone. He thinks I will be able to hear someone talk to me from miles away. I have read about them, but I will have to experience it to believe it.

Summer 1878

New inventions and ideas are happening all across America. Everyone is excited to experience them. Thomas L. is friends with the family who has the first talking machine in southwest Missouri.

April 23, 1880

I walked with Thomas L. today to the cross in the woods, his gift for me on the day he left to go on the Oregon Trail in 1845. For thirty-five years it has been my place of rest to find peace. In times when all I could do was cry, God heard what I could not utter the words to say. The cross is now worn on the sides where I held on to it to pray. Most everyone in the family has used it as a prayer altar.

My most favorite time to walk to the cross is when the May apples are in bloom. Today, the lovely, white blossoms brushed against my knees as my reminder I was nearing the cross. It will always feel like a walk in heaven.

I noticed Thomas L. walked slower than usual and was short of breath. He said he was fine. I asked him if he would tell me more about his travels west on the Oregon Trail.

He pulled out his hunting knife from the sheath attached to his belt, walked over to a tree, and carved a cross. He explained that was how he communicated with the Indians about God.

Then he told me something he had never shared with anyone else in the family. He told me about a beautiful lady he fell in love with. She had been traveling with her parents on the wagon train west. She hoped to one day be able to teach English to Indian children. He said she was quiet, and her sweet smile melted his heart. Her name was Sara Ann.

While they were traveling over the first small set of mountains, she fell from their wagon, hitting her head on a boulder. Thomas L. said she didn't bleed, but it must have caused a blood clot in her head. She first started with headaches that got so severe she could no longer ride in the wagon.

The wagons had to push forward to get over the mountains before the early snows started, so he stayed behind to care for Sara Ann. Her parents knew she was dying, and as difficult as it was, they left her in the arms of someone who loved her, Thomas L.. He said he held her close as she slowly became weaker, and the pain got worst. Before she died, she told him that she loved him.

He said he buried her near a small stream under a weeping-willow tree and that he dug white wild flowers and planted them on top of her grave. Then he carved a cross on the willow tree and her name under the cross. He knelt beside her grave and cried.

Thomas L. did not know that the Indians had been watching him from a distance while he cared for Sara Ann in her last days. Suddenly, the Indians came and surrounded him. They got down from their horses, and each one of them walked over and placed their hand on the cross on the willow tree and then put their hand on his shoulder. This was when they made a spiritual connection to understand God. When they saw from a distance how much he loved Sara Ann, they wanted to know the God that made him love so deeply.

Thomas L. told me this was why he went back year after year on the Oregon Trail, so he could visit her grave and see the Indians. He knew God had begun to open their hearts. The year after Sara Ann died, when he went to her grave, the Indians had built a white stone wall around where she was buried and had placed white feathers across the top of her grave. He went back each year to meet the Indians at her grave.

Then he told me he was too young to remember his father, John Catts, but how much he learned to love Thomas Crawford for accepting him as a son. Thomas had encouraged him to call him Papa and had taught him how to plant and care for apple trees. He said Papa had such a heart for God, and he showed him how to slice an apple across the core to find a star in the center of the apple. Thomas Crawford always said it was like the star over Bethlehem, the night Jesus was born. Thomas L. said that was how he taught the Indians the story of Jesus. And that he had planted apple trees for the Indians and carved crosses all along the Oregon Trail.

I reminded Thomas that his father always said, "When you see an act of love, you will feel the spirit of God."

We talked as we walked home through the white May apple blooms, out of the woods, and into a green field of sunshine. I thought it was like an afternoon in heaven with my dearly loved son, Thomas L.

April 23, 1880

Thomas L. had no idea that the cross in the woods had been used by so many as a place to find comfort. He knew it had been a meeting place for Jane Ann and Robert during the Civil War.

On his last walk to the cross with his mother, he was glad he told her about the woman he fell in love with on the Oregon Trail. And how her death had opened the hearts of the Indians.

The gift that he left for his mother to find was the same gift he left for the Indians to find. He had carved a cross on trees all along the trail to California.

Thomas L. peacefully died during the night from pneumonia. He was sixty-three years old and was buried beside his oldest brother, George, at the Catts/Crawford Cemetery. Fannie helped Frances carve a cross on a tree at the cemetery. She wanted it left behind for others to find in memory of her uncle Thomas.

Thomas L. had built each of his brother's caskets when they died. Now, he had no brothers to build his. Frances was happy when William Catts, her grandson, asked if he could build his uncle Thomas's casket. Her son's job was now passed to a new generation.

Spring 1881
The months after Thomas L. died, I felt so lonely. I had never experienced silence like this. When John and Thomas died, I had the children to care for and a business to build so I could provide for our family. After Thomas died, now over forty-years ago, young Thomas L. overnight became a man with responsibilities. When we homesteaded the land, I didn't realize he gave up his dreams so he could care for Charles and me. Even when he traveled on the Oregon Trail, he came home during the winters.

He cared for all of us after George died and while Robert was away during the war. I am ashamed I did not tell Thomas L. how important he was to our family. He was the glue that held us together.

Fannie has moved back to the farmhouse with me. She comes and goes to teach the children at the school in town. She makes me laugh when she tells me about the many things she hopes to do in her life and where she wants to go. Perhaps she actually will go to London one day to visit the Queen.

Spring 1881

The winter after Thomas L. died was hard for Frances. She thought about moving to town to be near Jane Ann or Mary Ann. But thinking they would be three lonely widows who missed their husbands, she instead wanted to stay at the farm.

Fannie moved to the farmhouse to be with her. Thinking of Fannie's future, Frances encouraged her granddaughter to think about building a new house on the west side of the farm.

CHAPTER 15

Summer 1887

Fannie has a long process ahead of her to build a house from the standing timber on the farm. From the porch, I can see the men unloading their misery whip saws from the wagon to begin working. The black oak trees are like old friends to me since I have watched them grow for almost fifty years.

The plan Fannie is working on will produce a good, sturdy house. The front will face south so she can see the pond from the porch. The fireplace will be on the north side of the house and will keep those rooms warm. The best and most beautiful spot will be the view from the west kitchen window. The evening sunset on the cemetery will remind us that as long as someone cares about those who have died, they will not be forgotten.

Summer 1887

Frances is delighted Fannie is going to build a new house so she will have a home of her own. The farm has always been a special place for her granddaughter. After she finished school in Virginia, the farm was the first place she lived. Charles had just died in California when she came home, so it was a good time to stay with her grandmother. They quickly became close.

September 1888

My last child has died. My caring and loving Jane Ann had been sick for just a few days. As I sat beside her bed, we talked about when we lived in Baltimore and what she remembered about her father, John Catts. She told me how excited she was to make me a pink hat for my birthday, so I would smile again. She told me, "John Neal died so suddenly from yellow fever, we all cried ourselves to sleep every night, missing him."

Then she said how happy she was when I fell in love with the handsome Mr. Crawford, Esq., adding, "And I was very happy he had such a handsome son named Robert."

We laughed about the snowball battle in the side yard and the Independence Day picnics. The days before she died, we talked about all the good times and never mentioned the challenging days during the war. She cried when she told me how much she missed Robert after he died. And we both cried when we talked about Charles, George, and Thomas L.

I sat with Jane Ann through the night and was with her when she died. I laid my head on her bed and cried as I thought how no mother should lose all of her children.

I wondered if God had forgotten me. I will go to the cross in the woods to cry.

September 1888

Jane Ann died at age seventy-five on September 6, 1888, with her ninety-six-year-old mother at her side. She was laid to rest beside her husband, Robert Crawford, at the Catts/Crawford Cemetery. The beautiful fall leaves made a quilt over their graves.

Spring 1889

Fannie stayed with me through the winter after Jane Ann died. When we came to the farm in 1839, we built a one-room cabin to live in for winter. Then we built the farm house we have lived in for twenty-three years, until the bushwhackers burned it to the ground in 1864.

We again built a one-room cabin to live in until a new house was built in 1866, after the war. We lived in that house for twenty-four years, and now my grandson, William, will live in the house. He wants to grow strawberries and is saving to buy a farm north of Mount Vernon.

Moving day was an exciting time for Fannie and me. We were so proud when we moved into the fine-looking two-story white house she built. I left the furniture William would need, and my other things I gave to Fannie. I kept my down-filled bed so the new house will feel like home. And my flat, down-filled pillow that I pulled the feathers from to make a pillow for little Clarence.

Also, I kept my rocking chair for the front porch. We can go out in the evenings to watch the pond across from the house.

I will keep the sign that John carved for me that Thomas attached to the wagon step with me until I die. The treasured words written by my beloved friend, Francis Scott Key, "In God is our trust," have given me confidence to go on in the toughest days. And I will set the wooden box containing the piece from the flag on the table beside my bed with our family Bible on top.

With our family Bible, my journal, my sign, my piece of the flag, and my family, I will finish my last days enjoying my memories. The Bible will keep our family records. My journal will tell my story.

And the cross in the woods I will leave for someone else to find.

I am so blessed. How could I ever ask God for more than He has given me?

Spring 1889

For some, a move would be hard, but for Fannie, moving became another adventure in life. Francis and Fannie moved into the house in the spring of 1989. The upstairs was finished in 1890.

April 1890

With my shaking ninety-eight-year-old hand, I will write for the last time in my journal. On my seventh birthday, my Mama gave me this journal. I wrote, "I will write the story of my life." And that is what I have done.

I choose to think that I have had a good life, filled with God's best blessings. I had two wonderful husbands, John Catts and Thomas Crawford. I had wonderful children, George, Jane Ann, John Neal, Thomas L., and Charles. I was also blessed with Robert and his three brothers. I have an abundance of wonderful grandchildren who have loved and cared for me.

I lived through the most exciting times in American history and experienced friendships that have lasted a lifetime. I have keepsakes that still touch my heart.

I have survived yellow fever, many wars, and even my home being burned to the ground. The saddest thought for me is that I have outlived all my children and many of my grandchildren. After Jane Ann died, I wondered why God let me keep living.

In my last hours, I think about what heaven will be like. Will the ones I love know me or will I know them? To find this out, I will have to wait until I get there.

I often thought that our earthly life was just a place to stop on our way home.

I can't wait to get home to heaven. I have waited a lifetime to meet the One who got me through this life.

April 1890

On a warm spring day, Frances wanted to go to the cross in the woods one last time. Fannie held her tiny, frail arm and helped her walk nearer to the cross. They walked through the white May apple blooms that were more beautiful than they had ever been. The sunlight twinkled down from heaven to illuminate the cross as Frances bowed one last time. Then she began to sing in a soft voice that echoed through the woods and up toward to heaven, "Amazing grace, how sweet the sound ..."

Frances Neal Catts Crawford peacefully died on April 24, 1890. Fannie and Mary Ann were at her side. She was buried in the family cemetery next to her son, Thomas L. Catts, on a beautiful spring day.

The hayfield was filled with people who came to pay their respects to the lady whose faith had not been silent.

The following year a street in Mount Vernon was named in her honor.

Fall 1890

The will of Frances Catts Crawford was read to her family a few months after she died but was not finalized until May 1892.

The first line states, "In the name of God, Amen," meaning her will was a declaration of truth.

Frances's first request in her will was for two-hundred dollars be given to the Mount Vernon Christian Church to further Christianity in Lawrence County.

Her first last wish, and perhaps her prayer, was for future generations. She knew her faith in God was her strength in life and her eternal future. That was her hope for the future generations.

Her farm that she loved was left in equal and fair shares to her grandchildren. Fannie was to be allowed to live on the farm in the house she built until her last days if she wanted.

Frances wanted the silver watch that belonged to her brother, John Neal, that had been given to her son, George, now to be given to his son, William Catts.

Her granddaughters were each given one-half dozen silver spoons with the letter "C." The remaining sets of silverware from the Catts and the Crawford families were to be divided equally among the grandchildren.

No one knew what happened to the piece from the Star-Spangled Banner flag—perhaps buried with Frances.

PART III

CHAPTER 16

"There are no more journal entries," Pops said as he looked up at Grams and Tate.

No one uttered a sound. Only silence filled the air in the room. A tear rolled down Grams' face, and Pops and Tate sat staring straight ahead.

Pops understood why Grams was crying. They had taken a long journey with Frances Neal Catts Crawford. She'd written the story of her life in her own words. And they had found her journal. They experienced her life from her eyes and through her heart and walked with her as she felt the joys and heartaches that seemed so unbalanced. Perhaps, she would've wanted less heartache and deserved more joy, but she instead accepted the life she was given. She didn't like the circumstances, but her soul was always at peace.

Tate shook his head and abruptly said, "We can't just let her die. No, she just can't die. She was our friend, and I don't want her to die."

Pops patted his grandson's arm. Perhaps, unknowingly, Tate was also talking about his friend, Rocky.

"But she did die, Tate." Pops softly said.

"But as long as someone remembers her," Grams said gently, "she will never be forgotten. So, what can we do so that Frances and her family are not forgotten? We clean their graves every year to remember them and respect their family."

With sadness in his heart, Pops shook his head as if he didn't know what they could do. Fumbling with the other books he had laid aside that had been with the journal in the dresser, he picked up the book, *Pilgrim's Progress*. He thumbed through it, as if he were hoping he would find something.

"We need a break," Pops announced. "Let's go for a walk in the woods, and maybe we'll see a new fawn in the thicket," Before they had even gotten off the porch, Tate began asking questions.

"Why did Frances have so much heartache in her life?" Tate asked. "It doesn't seem fair that she had so many family members die."

Such a deep question from someone so young. Pops wasn't surprised, though. Frances Catts's story was sad, even to him. "Tate, you need to learn at your young age that *fair* is where you go ride rides. It has nothing to do with life. God never wanted Frances or anyone to have heartache, but we are the ones who chose to go against God. He never promised us that life would be fair, only that he would be with us. The story of Job in the Bible is a good example of someone whose heartache was unbalanced. When everything was taken from him, only his faith in God tipped the scales."

"I know that story, Pops," Tate said. "But what helped Job or Frances get through the times when their hearts hurt really bad? And what stopped them from being mad at God?"

Realizing Tate was questioning his own faith in dealing with the death of his friend, Rocky, Pops knew Tate needed to talk. They walked around the pond and into the woods. Pops listened while Tate opened his heart about how much he missed Rocky and how unfair God had been by not letting him live.

"God could have healed him," Tate said, his angry voice echoing through the trees.

"Yes," Pops responded calmly. "Your faith has given you confidence that God could have healed him if he had chosen to. But your question is why God didn't heal him. That question is one we all ask sometime in our life. Weather it's you, Frances, or Job, our soul cries out for the answer. I know God loves Rocky more than you do, Tate. He didn't want to see him suffer any more than you did.

"With God, Frances was able to get through the pain of losing two husbands, her children, and her home. God wasn't the reason she lost everything, but with God she got through the losses.

"Remember when Frances said she was thankful for the time God allowed her to be married? And when Fannie Catts wrote her poem with a thankful heart rather than a bitter heart, she wrote, 'I believe it is God who chooses who will live and who will die. So, I choose to be thankful that love did not pass me by.'

"God knew Rocky would have cancer. And he knew when he would die, just as we all will, but he allowed Rocky to be your friend and to touch your life. We never get over losing someone we love. There will always be an empty spot when they are gone. But God promised he will be with us *always*." Pops put his arm over Tate's shoulder and pulled him close.

Pops looked up. They'd been so deep in their conversation, he hadn't noticed the white May apple blooms covering the ground ahead of them in the woods.

For the first time ever, Tate saw the fragrant white blooms. He bent down to take a whiff of them. How odd. They smelled more like lemons and not at all what he'd expected a flower in the woods to smell like. Then it dawned on him that these flowers were part of the clue as to where to find Frances's treasure.

"The cross must be here somewhere!" he suddenly shouted.

Tate ran ahead. The big turned-down May apple leaves brushed against the knees of his jeans as he searched for the cross in the woods. He and Pops looked wherever there were white blooms but didn't find the cross.

"You know, Tate," Pops said. "The probability of it still existing after all these years is small."

Tate hadn't thought of that, but after finding so many things that had been preserved, he believed the cross had to survive too. Pops continued to follow him as he searched.

A rabbit dove into a short brush pile ahead of him. "I want to see if there's a nest of baby bunnies," he said, hoping he'd get to see bunnies.

"Let's push the brush down," Pops said, "and I'll come back another time to clear it."

They pushed down and stepped on the brush. Then Tate thought he saw something closer to a tree. So, they pushed down more of the brush so they could get closer.

Tate stopped and stared, his heart beating with excitement. There in front of them stood the cross, aged and rugged looking, with moss growing over most of it.

They stood in silence.

At that moment, the sun's rays shined through the tall trees down on the cross. In awesome wonder at the sight, Tate walked closer and bowed down on one knee.

Pops put his hand on Tate's shoulder and bowed beside him.

Together, they prayed at the old rugged cross in the woods.

Walking back to the house, Tate realized his anger was gone.

When they came out of the woods, Grams was swinging on the porch and waving at them. She had something white in her hand.

They walked around the pond and through the white gate. As they walked up the lane to the house, she stood up and called for them to hurry.

Popes and Tate ran up on the porch, afraid something might have happened to Grams.

She reached out and handed Tate an envelope and said, "After you left to take a walk, I started picking things up, and this was on the floor beside the chair you were sitting in. It must have fallen out of a book when you were thumbing through it."

Pops looked over Tate's shoulder at what was written on the front of the envelope.

And they both said, "'My Last Years,' by Fannie M. Catts."

Grams had not opened the letter. She had waited for Tate and Pops. And she had made sweet peach tea and peach cobbler as a surprise to enjoy on the porch.

The three of them sat down on the porch. Tate carefully opened the envelope.

He unfolded the letter and began to read ...

To whomever finds this letter,

Out of respect for my grandmother, whom I miss with my whole heart, I, Fannie M. Catts, couldn't bring myself to write in her journal about my last years, so I decided to write down on paper a bit about my life after she passed away.

And my dear mother, Mary Ann, misses her even more than I do.

The quiet life at the farm has allowed me to awaken the dreams I had set aside for so many years. I wanted to experience life like never before. Seeing my school children excited about learning new things, inspired me to want to learn also.

I've read about the magnificent Carnegie Hall opening in New York City in May 1891 and hope to attend one day.

Also, Ellis Island will be opening in New York in 1892. Oh, there's so much I want to see in this big world.

I enjoy my life in the Ozarks. Last weekend, I ventured to Springfield with friends to see the boisterous Commercial Street. People were coming and going from the Frisco Train Station, and I got caught up in the hustle and bustle of it all. We rode the street car from Commercial Street to Doling Park. My friends and I paddled in small boats in the lake and went to Giboney Cave to feel the cool air from the underground spring.

My favorite enjoyment was the thrill of riding the Shoot-the-Chutes splash-down ride in the park. I rode it over and over and felt young again. We picnicked and listened to music at the bandstand and at the pavilion.

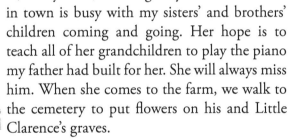

My mother, Mary Ann, is doing very well. Her house in town is busy with my sisters' and brothers' children coming and going. Her hope is to teach all of her grandchildren to play the piano my father had built for her. She will always miss him. When she comes to the farm, we walk to the cemetery to put flowers on his and Little Clarence's graves.

I shall write more sometime.

Teaching school in 1891

While teaching school in 1891, I decided to walk my class to Williams Springs, just down from the court house in Mount Vernon. The children loved the class I taught them about bugs and fish. I brought two fishing poles, one for the girls and one for the boys. They had a competition on who caught the most fish and could name what kind of fish they were.

Not long after this outing, I got in trouble with the principal at my school. I read about a new sport called basketball. It sounded like such fun, so I moved back the chairs and desks in my class room. I put an apple basket at each end of the room, and with a ball, we learned to play basketball. The principal thought perhaps the loud, aggressive sport should be banned. My mother also agreed since her many grandchildren then wanted to play basketball in her house.

I'd consider myself a healthy, vivacious teacher, church worker, and often an authority on many subjects, including medicine. Like my grandmother, Frances, I can recite full books from the Bible, and I adore poetry. I often sit on the porch in the evenings, writing poetry.

When I attend church with my mother, she gets upset with me for not looking at the Bible while the pastor reads Scripture. Instead, I say the Scripture along with him. She is feeling good for now, but winter is always a challenge for her health.

I so love teaching at the Mount Vernon Academy. I hope that I will not get in trouble with the principal as often here.

About Harold Bell Wright

In 1896, we got an interesting new part-time pastor, writer, and house painter named Harold Bell Wright. He will also be teaching at the school this year. After he volunteered to preach at the First Christian Church, Pierce City soon hired him as a pastor there. He teaches school during the week and rides his horse to Pierce City to preach on Sundays. He and I have become good friends.

He often talks about when he first came to the Ozarks due to health reasons. The relaxing life along the White River and the beauty of the Ozark Mountains captivated him.

One summer while fishing and camping along the river, heavy rains caused the river to flood. While looking for a place to stay, he met John and Anna Ross. They invited him to stay with them in their log cabin. Fascinated with their way of living, he visited them as often as possible.

The following summer, Harold asked me to go by wagon to Branson to stay with his friends. They opened their cabin to me as they'd been doing for Harold. Not far from the cabin was one of the largest caves ever found in Missouri—Marble Cave. They offered tours to those who were brave enough to go down into the deep, dark unknown.

I was excited to go. I carried the lantern and walked between John and Anna as we entered into the large cave entry room. It was so big, they call it the Cathedral Room. As we stepped deeper into the cave, hundreds of bats suddenly flew up from the deep abyss. My heart raced for a moment, but then we kept going and went as far into the cave as we were allowed to go. With a torch held high, Harold led us back up to the top.

The following year Harold accepted a preaching job at Pittsburg, Kansas. We kept in touch throughout the years at Christmas.

Ice skating in the pond

The record temperature on February 12, 1899, was minus twenty-nine degrees. I couldn't contain myself, so I dressed in as many layers as I could and went ice skating on the pond in front of the house. I'm sure people would say I was crazy for doing that, but I enjoyed the freedom of gliding through the freezing air as icicles formed on my scarf near my nose. I had a delightful time. I don't think I ever told my sweet mother about ice skating on the pond. It might keep her awake at night with worry.

The Missouri State Fair

I and a couple friends went to Sedalia, Missouri, to the first Missouri State Fair on September 9, 1901. Oh, what a lovely day. The weather cooperated and gave us a fine fall day. I sipped Coca-Cola and sampled so many delicious foods. I had high hopes that I might ride a bull; however, the rules were very specific. No women allowed.

The St. Louis 1904 World's Fair

For over a year, I've been planning on attending the upcoming Louisiana Purchase Exposition, informally known as the St. Louis 1904 World's Fair, an international exposition being held to commemorate the centennial of the Louisiana Purchase. I wanted to go alone so that no one would slow me down.

I took the Frisco train from Mount Vernon to Springfield and on to the beautiful Saint Louis Union Station. I rode by carriage to my hotel. For dinner, I excitedly strolled down to see my first look at the World's Fair.

I walked around in amazement at the sights I could have never imagined could be so beautiful. Tired and hungry, I sat on a bench in front of the Westinghouse Electric Auditorium and ate something new called a hamburger and drank a new soda drink called Dr. Pepper. A nice man in a hat came and sat with me to have his first Dr. Pepper also. We talked while we enjoyed our soda.

When he stood up to leave, he tipped his gray hat and said, "My name is Thomas Edison, and it was a pleasure to visit with you, my dear."

I was stunned and wish he'd have told who he was sooner. Although, if he had we probably wouldn't have had such a leisurely talk.

I then tried a new way to eat ice cream. Instead of in a bowl, it was served in a thin waffle rolled into a cone. As I walked around and saw the Palace of Fine Art, where the Olympics would be played, the Nations on Display, the huge bird cage at the Saint Louis Zoo Park, and more people than I've seen my entire life. The exhibits and the beauty of the buildings captivated me.

After hearing "Stars and Stripes Forever," a concert directed by John Philip Sousa, I waited afterward to meet the conductor. Walking down the side steps from the stage, he greeted me at the bottom. I asked him if he remembered my brother, William Catts, who played in his brass band in years past.

Smiling, he said, "Of course, I remember William. He was a good musician and should have stayed in music. He would still be with my band."

In only seven days, I felt like I had experienced it all. On my train ride home, I sat next to an interesting young man named Harry Truman. He was going to Springfield to visit a friend before returning home to Lamar, Missouri.

This was a trip to remember always.

Thinking about my mother

I see my mother slowing down more each year. She has always been kind and sweet to everyone. Some call her, "The grand old lady." I hope they mean it as a compliment. Family has been her life. She is content and happy as long as she has loved ones to visit her. I remember how proud she was the day she returned the county money she found buried in the rose garden. She was clear that she wanted the deposit to the county made in the name of George N. Catts, deceased. She cleared his name for the entire family.

Typhoid fever and smallpox.

In 1906, The Sisters of Mercy opened Saint Johns, a new forty-bed hospital in Springfield. When typhoid fever and smallpox was at its worst, the Sisters set up a camp outside of town to keep it from spreading. The sick were picked up by wagons and taken to the fever camps for treatment. When disease hit, schools were closed, and people stayed in their homes.

I remember that many people died from the fevers, including my father. So, I wanted to help. I rode the train from Mount Vernon to Springfield once a week to volunteer at the hospital.

The Missouri State Sanatorium was built on Chigger Hill, in Mount Vernon in 1907, to treat tuberculosis, also known as the "White Plague." After this hospital opened, I volunteered there instead of going to Springfield.

A surprise

I got a surprise in the mail today. My friend Harold Bell Wright sent me a book he'd written, "The Shepherd of the Hills," telling about the life of Old Matt and Aunt Mollie living in Old Matt's Cabin above the White River. The characters were based on his dear friends, John and Anna Ross. He sent me a first-edition, signed copy of his book. I love the story and will treasure this gift.

I showed it to my mother and let her be the first to read it.

My walk down memory lane

I haven't written anything for a few years, but I was feeling particularly lonely one day, so I took a walk down memory lane and thought I'd write down my thoughts.

One evening while looking through my cedar chest at my many keepsakes, I found twelve quilt blocks. Twelve of my dearest friends had each made one quilt block as a gift for me when I left Virginia in 1858. Each block was embroidered with a flower and my friends' names. Realizing I had never pieced them together as a quilt, I started sewing. I sewed light green cotton strips between the blocks to form the quilt. Across the bottom in pink letters I embroidered, "Make new friends, but keep the old. One is silver and the other is gold." I had a feeling of pride to have finished my "Friendship Quilt" after so many years.

This inspired me to sort through the things my mother had given me and that my grandmother, Frances, had left at the house. I found the wooden tool box that had actually been a fishing box from my grandmother's bother, John Neal. He had given it to my uncle Thomas L. the last time he took him fishing before going to London. Uncle Thomas L. later used it as a tool box.

I opened it, sorted his keepsakes, and laid them inside the box. Then I placed the wooden sign grandfather John Catts had carved in 1814 on top of everything. Thinking how much my grandmother loved the sign, I touched the words that are forever written in my memory and on my heart, "In God is our trust." I laid his Bible on top of the sign, closed the lid, put a lock on it, and set it in the back corner of the attic.

I found a saddlebag with treasures inside that had belonged to Uncle Robert Crawford. In the back pouch of the bag, I found a key and a round, black, metal ball. I opened the bag and laid out his items on a table. He had legal documents, a razor, a billfold, and a soldier's Bible with a round hole near the top. So many stories about Uncle Robert came to mind and how he helped many people during the war. I put his items back in the saddle bag, locked it, and hung it from a hook hanging from a rafter in the attic.

Grandmother Frances had left the camelback trunk she brought from Virginia in the house. It had belonged to her mother, and she gave it to her daughter, my aunt Jane Ann, who stored the trunk upstairs. Some of her things had been left in the trunk so they were given back to her after Aunt Jane Ann passed away.

I opened the trunk, and lying on top was a sign that read, "Catts Fine Millinery Shop." Laying it aside, I lifted out a quilt Jane Ann had given to her mother, my grandmother, on the day she took possession of the farm in 1839. It was called a crazy quilt, made from fabric scraps.

Digging deeper, I found a metal box with a rope design. It had a small lock, and the key was tied to the lock with a piece of yarn. When I unlocked the box and looked inside, I found a pair of black gloves with the initials J. A. C. I put all of Aunt Jane Ann's treasures in the metal box and locked it. I kept the key, then placed the box in the bottom of the trunk with other boxes. I laid the quilt and the sign on top.

I closed the trunk and sat down on it for a few moments, smiling as I thought about how kind Aunt Jane Ann had been. I pushed the trunk inside the attic and stacked hat boxes on top of it.

Then I got out a key to a suitcase my mama, Mary Ann, had left for me. Pulling it out from under my bed, I unlocked it and lifted the top of the suitcase, and there was the cash box my Papa, George Catts, had buried in the rose garden before he left to go to the battle at Wilson Creek. Opening it, I saw the sign that sat on his desk, "George Neal Catts, County Treasurer, Lawrence County Missouri." Also in the suitcase was a black ledger embossed with "Mount Vernon Mercantile." I remembered how Mama had struggled to keep it open after my Papa died.

Wedged in the corner was a cherrywood box with a heart carved on top. Inside the heart on the box were the same words Papa had carved on the piano for my mother. "To my sweet Mary Ann." On the corner were the initials, G.C. and M.A. and underneath was carved, "Forever." I didn't want to cry, and instead, I turned my thoughts to good times I had as a child.

When I opened the lid, laying on top of some letters tied with a faded ribbon was a lock and key set. Setting them aside, I took out a blue baby sweater and hat. Aunt Jane Ann had crocheted them for my brother, little Clarence. A tear rolled down my face as I thought about not being able to be at his funeral. Underneath the sweater and hat was a white plate—the one Mama sat at the head of the table for Father all those years.

I put the treasures back in the box and put everything in the suitcase and pushed it under my bed.

Mama

My mama, Mary Ann, had enjoyed good health for several years, but her inflammatory rheumatism now caused her much pain. I would go into town to sit at her bedside, and we would talk about good times with family. Seeing her getting weaker, I got out the silver heart-shaped locket from her china music box. She showed me the tiny picture of Papa. Mama held it tightly in her hand. I picked up the music box and turned the stem. It played, "Mary Had A Little Lamb."

I held my Mama's hand as she closed her eyes for the last time and passed away peacefully on July 19, 1910.

William built a very nice coffin for our mother, and she was laid to rest beside the love of her life, George Catts. Her obituary said, "She was a splendid woman of a kind and loving disposition."

My sisters and brothers wanted me to have the heart-shaped locket and music box.

It has been several months since Mama passed away. The day is cool and the air crisp. I'd been missing my parents and grandmother. So, I walked to the cross in the woods. The fall leaves covering the ground made a carpet for me to walk on. I thought about the many times I came here with Grandmother.

I kneeled at the cross and thanked God for the family he had given to me to love. Then I started my walk home. I stopped and closed my eyes for a moment. I could almost smell the May apple blooms. After I got home, I cooked supper and sat at the table by myself, as I did every night. Glancing out the west kitchen window. I could see the day was almost gone. I stood in the kitchen and watched as the sun melted away over the cemetery in the hayfield.

Leaving the dishes until later, I went to my room and pulled the suitcase from underneath the bed and set it on the mattress. I got out the cherrywood box and wrapped the white plate in the blue sweater. I placed Mama's silver locket back in her music box and wrapped it with the blue baby hat.

Gently, I laid the letters inside the box, closed the lid, and put the lock on the box. Then I straightened the things in the suitcase, closed the top, and locked it too, taking a moment to rub my hand over the letters G.N.C. on the suitcase.

With an oil lamp in one hand and the suitcase in the other, I slowly walked up the wooden steps through the bedroom and opened the attic door. I tucked the suitcase in a corner, but I must have bumped the music box, as it began to play, "Mary Had A Little Lamb."

Before my mother died, she filled in all the family records in the Catts Family Bible and gave it to me in the wooden box Uncle Thomas L. made for her. He had carved the cross on the top. I filled in the date she passed away, took it upstairs, and laid it on a dresser. After my grandmother died, I kept her journal and some other books in the side door of the old tiger oak dresser upstairs.

Then I went down to my room and opened my cedar hope chest, lifted out the white lace wedding dress I never got to wear, and draped it over the bed. I opened the lace purse and took out the poem I had written almost fifty years before and read it.

With a huge smile, I read out loud the last couple lines. "But I believe it is God who chooses who will live and who will die, So, I choose to be thankful that love did not pass me by." I sighed and held it to my heart for a moment and remembered the love I once shared.

Then I picked up the book, "Shepherd of the Hills." Flipping to the back, I gazed at the pictures of my friend, Harold Bell Wright with me and the school children. I took everything out of the hope chest and laid them on my bed. Each item took me to a different memory, and I savored them all.

Tired, I laid down on my bed and pulled the friendship quilt up over me, falling asleep surrounded by my memories.

The next morning, I folded each item and carefully placed them in the hope chest. Then I put the keys I'd gathered and a brass key ring from the desk in my pocket. Before breakfast, I opened the stairway door and step by step carried the chest up the wooden stairs. Tired when I got to the top, I sat down for a few minutes to catch my breath.

The sun was just coming up, so I walked over to the west window and looked out. A hazy morning fog hung over the cemetery as it did many mornings in Missouri.

I locked my hope chest, opened the attic door, and pushed it inside over against a low wall. Taking the family Bible from the dresser, I sat down on the bed and looked at it one last time then put it back in the box with the cross carved on top and laid it on a box inside the attic.

My date of death will be the only one not yet written in the Bible.

I went into the other bedroom and opened the side door of the old dresser. I took out my grandmother's journal and looked at it one last time. I sat on the bed and put the seven keys on the brass key ring from the desk.

I sat a while longer, thinking about the wonderful life I've had. I then went into the west bedroom and stood looking at the cemetery one last time.

I will fold this letter and put it in one of my grandmother's favorite books, "Pilgrims Progress." I will then lock the dresser door.

Then I will hide the seven keys in the gray stone chimney in the attic. I will now end my long letter about the last few years of my mother's life and mine. I have had such a good life and I am forever thankful for the family God gave me to love.

I am leaving someone a gift, but they will have to find it,
Fannie M. Catts
December 1, 1910

Tate, Grams and Pops were again silent. They found a copy of Fannie's obituary that showed the date she died. Tate read the clipping to his grandparents. "Fannie Catts passed away in her home at the farm, December 7, 1910. Her sister sat by her bedside as she closed her eyes one last time. She was seventy years old and was buried beside her Mama in the family cemetery in the hayfield. On the bottom of her gravestone were the words, 'She hath done all that she could.'"

EPILOGUE

2018, Mt. Vernon, Missouri

"Every one of them died," Tate said, his freckled face looking sad.

This had been a rich but difficult experience for Pops' grandson. "Yes, they did die, Tate," he said. "But the best thing we can do is to never forget Frances or her life."

"What can we do to never forget her?" Tate asked. "And how can we honor her for what she and her family did in wars and helping people. What can we do?"

"We clean her grave every year, Tate." Grams reminded him. "Until you asked who and why, she was just someone we didn't know, who was buried in our hayfield." She paused a moment. "But now we know her and Thomas L. and Robert and Jane Ann. And we know Mary Ann always loved George. And we know Fannie went into the same cave I've gone in and read some of the books I've read. They were real people, and I got to know them."

Tate suddenly sat up straight, a gleam in his eye and a smile on his face. "I think we should have a party or a celebration! And we could invite other people to learn about who they were and how they came here to homestead."

"The flag was so important to Frances. You know, we could put a flag pole at the cemetery," Pops announced excitedly.

"Yeah!" Tate agreed. "And we could sing 'The Star-Spangled Banner'."

Grams added, "You and Pops could carve a sign that says, *In God is our trust.*"

Pops grinned in pride as he thought about how much they had learned from Tate's two simple questions. "Yes, let's get started planning a celebration everyone will remember."

"When I get home," Tate added, "I'm going to plan a celebration for Rocky too."

And they all started talking at once, brimming with ideas and plans to honor the people buried in their hayfield.

Our life is like a puzzle. Each day creates a new piece.
Only God chooses when He puts the last piece in place.
—Billie Fulton

ABOUT THE AUTHOR

Billie Fulton, a writer from Springfield, Missouri, believes our first response to circumstances is always our heart response. Who we are in our heart comes out when faced with split-second decisions. After raising her family and spending years working in Women's Ministry in her church, she is following her dream to write about the hearts of real people in real times. She finds the challenges they faced, or that we face, are no different than people in the Bible. But as with them, our heart response to failure or success is how we learn. She is teaming with the love of her life, John Fulton, an accomplished artist, to visually compliment her writing. She treasures their time together and always finds time to dance in the bubbles with her grandchildren.

ABOUT THE ILLUSTRATOR

John Fulton is an accomplished watercolor artist from Springfield, Missouri. His commissioned collage paintings hang in both corporate and private collections nationally and internationally.

His unique style of visually displaying the heritage and attributes of a corporation or organization has allowed his work to be used on book covers, brochures, and limited edition prints. He most enjoys using his God given talent to illustrate books with his wife Billie.